The Dreams of Hannah Williams

Linda Ford

D1411567

Heartsong Presents

To my special, dear friend Brenda who has encouraged me, prayed for me, and shared coffee with me for more years than either of us cares to admit. May God continue to bless you in every way.

A note from the Author:
I love to hear from my readers! You may correspond with me by writing:

Linda Ford
Author Relations
PO Box 721
Uhrichsville, OH 44683

ISBN 978-1-59789-891-1

THE DREAMS OF HANNAH WILLIAMS

All scripture quotations are taken from the King James Version of the Bible.

All of the characters and events in this book are fictitious. Any resemblance to actual persons, living or dead, or to actual events is purely coincidental.

Our mission is to publish and distribute inspirational products offering exceptional value and biblical encouragement to the masses.

PRINTED IN THE U.S.A.

one

Hannah Williams felt the ground shake, then heard noise like thunder off the hills, followed by the pungent odor of hundreds of overheated bovine bodies. By the time the air filled with dust, she stood with her nose pressed to the window, watching cows stream down the street toward the holding pens at the rail yard. She shivered at the sheer number of them, their bulk. If they happened to decide to crash to the sidewalk and push into her premises. . .

She glimpsed cowboys astride horses. Some rode beside the herd; several more brought up the rear. They seemed to know how to control the animals, though she couldn't imagine how anyone could contain that tide of flesh.

As soon as the melee passed, she hurried outside. She didn't intend to miss the thrill of watching the cowboys corral this wild herd.

A group of excited boys jostled her as she hesitated several yards from the penning area. An exciting tension trickled across her spine at the noise of the cows pushing and bawling a protest against these strange surroundings, almost drowning out the sounds of men calling to each other and to the animals.

Nearby, a man on a big bay horse waved his arm in a circle, and several cowboys rode around the edge of the herd, turning them steadily toward the open pens at the end of the street. The cows hesitated. The man jerked his hand upward, and one of the cowboys edged toward the lead cows balking at the gate.

Suddenly, several animals bolted and the whole herd stampeded toward her. She pressed back against the wall of the nearest building, sucked in her breath to make herself smaller, and prayed the animals would miss her.

The big cowboy bellowed at the others then galloped toward her. He waved his hat at the animals and turned them toward the pens. The lead cows again hesitated at the gate then burst through, and like a flood, the rest followed.

The man who'd saved her from certain destruction rode to the gate, pushed it shut, then called to the others who gathered round him. He sat tall and big in the saddle, he and his horse moving as one body. He wore a black leather vest over a dusty gray work shirt. Like the other cowboys, he wore a red bandanna knotted around his neck. He said a few words to the other men. The way a couple of them hung their heads, Hannah guessed they'd been scolded. Two cowboys reined around and circled the pens. The others headed down the street. Hannah expected they would be looking for a bath, a hot meal, and a cold drink, not necessarily in that order. As they cantered by, she couldn't help thinking many of them looked more like boys than men.

"Ma'am?"

She jerked around to see the big man at her side. He doffed his hat. His dark brown eyes twinkled. "First time you've seen cattle moved through town?"

"First time I've seen cows so close. I thought I would be trampled. Thank you for saving me."

He swung his leg over the saddle horn and landed neatly

on both feet, then banged his black cowboy hat on his thigh, dislodging a cloud of gray dust. "You were never in any real danger. I made sure of that."

This was the closest she'd been to a cowboy, and she studied him. "You're the head cowboy?"

"You could say that. I own all these steers. Jake Sperling." He nodded almost formally.

She'd heard the Sperling name. Biggest landowners in the area. A powerful family who controlled much of the business around the cattle industry. And this was Jake, the owner. She'd heard rumors indicating he carried his power and authority like a badge, expecting others to honor them as much as he did. In fact, she'd heard he acted like he was the cream on the milk.

"I'm Hannah Williams." If she had to venture a guess, she would say he was not yet thirty, young to be in such a position. But then what did she know about when men in the West learned to control others? Maybe some were born to it. She only knew she intended to stay as far away as humanly possible from men who had such aspirations and ability. And opportunity. Living with her stepfather had taught her that lesson well.

But her curiosity overcame her caution. "What happens to all these animals now? Where do they go?"

He jerked to his full height. "Allow me to show you." He turned back toward the pens, the horse clopping on his heels.

Hannah hesitated a fraction of a second, considering the need to get back to work, even more briefly reminding herself she wanted nothing to do with men who exuded authority. But she did want to see how the cattle were handled, and he'd offered. No harm in that. It's not like she intended to give him any right to order her about. She fell into step beside him, hurrying a little to keep up with his long strides as she picked her way across the dusty street, carefully avoiding the steaming odorous piles left by the cows.

In the three weeks since her arrival in this cow town at the end of the railway, she'd glimpsed a way of life that appealed to her. Men were men. But women were given rights not expected back East. A single woman could even file a homestead claim.

Hannah smiled. She could imagine what Otto, her stepfather, would have to say about that. Her smile flattened. How could Mother have married a man so diametrically opposite to Hannah's father? Her father had been dead almost four years, but even though she was twenty-one and all grown up, Hannah still missed him so much. He would be happy to see Hannah finally had a way to be independent. He'd always encouraged her in that direction.

Jake went right to the wooden rails of the fence and leaned over, not a bit intimidated by the press of animals. Of course he wasn't. He worked with them daily.

But this was the first time she'd been close enough to a cow to touch it—if she had such an inclination, which she most certainly did not. The animals were even larger and more frightening close up. One animal tossed its head, rolling red, wild eyes and spraying slobber. Hannah gasped and backed several feet from the fence.

Jake laughed. "They can't hurt you. See." He reached over and patted one on the rump. The animal snorted and pushed away, causing even more commotion in the herd.

"I can see well enough from here." *And smell too well.* But determined not to show any weakness, she forced herself to the fence and leaned her arms on the rails as if feeling not a bit of trepidation.

The man grinned at her. "You should see it when a couple more herds arrive and all the pens are full."

"I can't imagine the noise." She grimaced. "Or the odor. How long do you keep them here?"

"As soon as the buyers see them, we cut a deal, load them on the railcars, and ship them east." He pushed away from the fence and stared hard at the station as if the building itself had done something to offend him. "I expected the buyers to be Johnny-on-the-spot. They better show up on the next train or they'll have some hard explaining to do. I can't afford to keep these steers standing around any longer than necessary."

She chose to ignore his dire comments. "I can't imagine how you get these wild things to march into railcars."

"No problem. We chase 'em up the ramp. You just have to know what you're doing."

Three boys ran past, screaming like banshees. The cows crashed into each other in their attempt to escape this frightening racket. The far fence creaked a protest.

Jake clambered up the rails. "Look out, boys," he called. "Hold 'em back."

The two patrolling cowboys raced to the troubled spot and drove the cattle back.

Jake slammed his hat on his head. "Keep your mind on business. I don't want to have to round up this bunch again. If they get out, you can bet it'll mean your jobs."

The two sketched salutes and looked scared half to death.

Hannah wanted to protest. They could hardly be blamed for some noisy children.

"Thank you for explaining it to me," she said, her words much softer than her heart. She had a distinct dislike for people holding power over others. In her mind, each person—male or female, young or old—should make his or her own decisions in life. And under God's control only. Not under the whims of another person who was stronger or had more power.

As she turned to walk away, Jake wrapped the reins of his horse around the top rail and followed. "Would you care to join me for dinner this evening?"

His grin invited her even more than his words, but she'd had her share of men with power—real or imagined. Otto had been more than enough. "I'm sorry. I'm a working girl. I seldom have time to get away." She increased her pace. "In fact, I'd better get back."

Jake slowed, let her hurry on, and then called, "Where do you work? When are you done for the day?"

She slowed, turned to face him, saw his wide smile, and almost wished she didn't have to work. If only he were a regular cowboy and not the powerful owner, she might consider taking a few hours away from the demands of her job. "I really have very little time off right now. I'm just trying to get my business operating." She wouldn't tell him where she actually worked—in the burned-out hotel two doors from the general store, next to a law office on one side, a vacant lot on the other. Not that she thought he'd bother looking her up, but she couldn't take the chance. The last thing she needed was someone who might be a prospective guest showing up before she was ready to reopen.

"I'll see you around," he said.

As she hurried back to the hotel, she wasn't sure if his

words were a promise or an order. Nor why it mattered.

She paused outside the Sunshine Hotel. What had her grandparents been thinking to name it that? The eternal optimists, always expecting sunshine and roses on their pathway. She hoped they were finding exactly that in California where they'd gone in search of more adventure.

When her grandparents had given her this hotel in Quinten, Dakota Territory, it had been an answer to prayer. A way to escape her controlling stepfather and establish her independence. She paused to silently thank God. But between her grandparents' departure and her arrival, the hotel had suffered a fire in the dining room, leaving the room with a hole in the middle of the floor and most of the rooms smoke damaged. Without money to hire a crew to do the cleaning and repairing, Hannah had little choice but to do the job herself.

She'd scrubbed the front windows until they gleamed, scoured the mud and water stains off the sidewalk, and managed to clean the door. But only a new coat of paint would successfully hide the water damage.

She pushed her way inside and adjusted the CLOSED FOR REPAIRS sign so it could be read from the outside. After much elbow grease on her part, the lobby was almost presentable. She'd managed to remove most of the water and smoke damage, but again, only paint would fix the wall next to the dining room. "Mort," she called. "Are you here?"

The long, cadaverous man who seemed to be part of the gift from her grandparents slouched into the room. "Where you been, miss?"

"I was watching the cattle being driven to the rail yards."

"Now you'll have to dust everything again." He nodded

toward the walnut table in the lobby she'd spent hours cleaning.

"Did you get the drapes down?" She'd given him instructions to remove the drapes in the back room where she slept. The smell was almost overpowering. She couldn't afford to have them professionally cleaned or replaced, but perhaps hanging them outside for a few days would air them out. In the meantime, she'd tack a sheet over the window for privacy.

"Took 'em down. Hung 'em outside like you said. But if you ask me, the best you can do is burn 'em and buy new ones."

"Yes, that would be nice, but I can't afford it. Is there lots of hot water?" If she scrubbed the wall next to the dining room one more time, perhaps she'd get rid of the smoke stains.

"Boilers are full. Still got to clean the chairs like you asked."

"Fine." It was like moving mountains to get Mort to go faster than a crawl, but grateful for his help with hauling water and moving the heavier stuff, she wasn't about to complain.

A little while later, she perched atop a ladder, scrubbing at the wall, her nostrils protesting at the smell. For the most part, the overpowering odor had disappeared from the room except when she got the walls wet.

As she scrubbed, she tried to plan when she could open. The work took much longer than she expected. So far she'd managed to do the lobby and the big suite of rooms in the corner upstairs, hoping, she supposed, at some point she could have guests and start to get a little money. Enough to pay Mort and buy paint would be a nice start. But somehow she had to first get enough to fix the huge hole in the middle of the dining room floor and replace the drapes in there.

Nothing could be done to salvage them. And the sooner she got them all down and burned, the sooner she'd get rid of that acrid smell. But Mort moved at his own pace. If they weren't so heavy, she'd do it herself.

She didn't look up when the door opened. Mort must have gone out for something and decided to use the front door rather than go around outside again.

When someone smacked the bell on the desk, she practically fell off her ladder. A woman cleared her throat.

"I'm sorry," Hannah said, righting herself. "We're not open for business at this point."

The woman tugged at her gloves. "Surely you can't be serious."

Hannah climbed off the ladder and headed for the desk. "We've had a fire. I'm still trying to clean up." She waved her hand around to indicate the work in progress.

The woman gave a dismissive glance. "But I always stay here." She drummed her fingers on the desk as if to let Hannah know she might as well quit stalling.

"I'm really very sorry, but I'm not prepared for guests."

"You? Maude and Harvey own this establishment. Where are they?"

"My grandparents. They've gone to California and left me the hotel."

"They left?" She looked about. "Well, I will miss them, but I wish them all the best."

"You knew my grandparents?" Well, of course she knew who they were. That wasn't what Hannah meant. It sounded like this woman knew them as more than businesspeople.

"Maude was always so good to visit with when I came to town." The woman marched toward the dining room. "We would sit in here for—oh my. Seems you've had a disaster."

"A fire," Hannah repeated.

The woman stared for another moment then returned to the desk. "Well never mind. We can get along without the dining room. But I can't imagine staying anywhere else. All the other hotels will be crowded with noisy cowboys coming and going at all hours." She placed her gloves beside Hannah's clasped hands and leaned toward her. "I'm sure you can find something suitable for a few nights. Can't you, my dear?"

Hannah looked into brown eyes and sensed the gentleness hid a steely determination. She admired the woman's perseverance, but she really wasn't ready for guests. Didn't know when she would be, in fact. But she was tempted. After all, there was the little problem of finances.

The door flung open again. Could no one read the sign? Closed for repairs meant closed.

She blinked as Jake strode across the room, his boots thudding on the floor. She'd been forced to throw out most of the carpeting, destroyed by mud, water, and smoke, but the boards had polished up nicely if somewhat reluctantly. How had he located her? And why?

He nodded at her before he turned to the other woman. "Mother, what are you doing here? Didn't you see the sign?" He turned to Hannah. "I'm sorry."

Hannah nodded, not knowing if he meant sorry his mother had ignored the sign or sorry she owned this damaged hotel. But before she could respond, Mrs. Sperling pressed her hand to her forehead and moaned. Her legs crumpled under her.

Jake swept her into his arms and looked around for a place to lay her. Hannah hurried over and put a cushion at the end of the sofa she'd cleaned and prayed it didn't still smell like smoke.

Mrs. Sperling's eyelids fluttered. "I'm sorry," she whispered.

Jake rubbed her hands and looked worried. "Mother, I told you to take it easy. You didn't have to come to town. I can conduct the business on my own."

Hannah watched the broad hands gentle the smaller, paler ones and remembered her father encouraging her in much the same way. He'd warmed her hands many times when she'd stayed outside too long or sat up too late trying to memorize her schoolwork. But more than his touch, she remembered his words, "Hannah, my daughter, you can do anything you put your mind to."

The picture inside her head changed. She and her father had been in his store, helping customers. A young man had come in with his mother, speaking so rudely to the woman he'd brought tears to her eyes. Her father waited until they left then said, "Hannah, you can tell a lot about a man by the way he treats his mother. Pay attention to that. It's the same way he'll treat his wife."

Hannah was certain Jake expected complete compliance from the men who worked for him. She remembered the way he'd spoken of the buyers and knew he'd accept no nonsense from men he did business with, either. But if her father was correct, Jake had a tenderness toward his family.

His mother spoke. "You can handle the business. I only came to help spend the money once the business is complete." She pushed up on her elbow. "I need a new dress and some material for new curtains and. . ."

Jake straightened and frowned at his mother.

The older woman fell back against the cushion and draped

her arm over her forehead. "Though I don't know how I'll manage it all. I should have insisted Audrey accompany me." Her voice was as thin as thread.

Jake groaned. "No doubt she'd bring the boys."

"Of course. Why should you mind? They're sweet and well behaved."

Jake sputtered.

Ignoring him, his mother explained to Hannah. "Audrey is my daughter, and she has two little boys."

"Mother, pull yourself together. We have to find rooms."

Hannah stared as the woman pressed her palm to her chest. "I'm feeling a little breathless. I'm just too exhausted to find someplace else." She waited until her son turned away then winked at Hannah.

Hannah almost choked holding back her laughter. Jake might be powerful, obeyed as the boss, but his mother played by her own rules, something Hannah admired.

Jake strode to the dining room door. "This isn't going to be fixed anytime soon."

"I'm sure Miss. . ." Mrs. Sperling smiled gently. "I'm sorry, dear, I don't believe you told me your name."

"Hannah Williams."

"Well, Miss Williams, I'm sure you can find us something, can't you?"

"The dining room—" Jake protested.

"We can eat anywhere we want. But I want to stay here." The older woman's voice began strong and then, as if she'd remembered her fragile condition, grew weaker. "I've always stayed here, and it just wouldn't feel right if I didn't."

"Mother, you'll just have to accept—"

Hannah decided then and there a woman so determined to

exert her independence should be accommodated. "The suite in the corner upstairs is ready for occupancy. I could let you have it, but, as you can see, there will be no dining available."

The woman sighed. "Thank you. I'm sure we'll be very comfortable."

Jake's expression darkened. He shot Hannah a look of accusation then faced his mother. "Mother, this is absurd. There are plenty of rooms available in town."

"But Miss Williams has just offered us rooms here."

Jake glowered at his mother. Hannah felt the familiar and unwelcome tightening in the pit of her stomach—the same feeling she got when she'd somehow challenged Otto's authority. Often she didn't even know what she'd done. Her father had encouraged the very things that brought on Otto's disapproval, so Hannah was left inadvertently crossing him on many occasions. His anger frightened her. She feared she would drive him to violence. But his sullen silence was even more frightening. It left her wondering when he'd finally punish her and how.

How would Jake deal with being challenged? He exuded power and control in a way that made Otto look insipid. Was Jake the same? Would he demand obedience from his mother? Insist on it? Send her silent messages promising to deal with this matter later—in private?

Mother and son confronted each other. Pressing her advantage, Mrs. Sperling patted her cheeks and managed to look weak and helpless. Something—Hannah was convinced—completely fabricated. Jake continued to look ready to grab his mother and stalk out the door.

Hannah stepped aside, realizing she'd unconsciously moved out of his way, expecting him to mow down anything and anyone in his path.

She jumped when Jake let out an explosion of air. "Very well, but it's going to be inconvenient to say the least." He stalked to the door.

Hannah blinked at his departing back.

Mrs. Sperling bounced to her feet. "My bags are at the livery," she called to her son.

Hannah pulled her thoughts together as best she could, still barely believing Jake had given in so easily. Or had he? Was it just for show? "Aren't you afraid of making him angry?" She gasped. "I'm sorry. That was inappropriate of me."

But Mrs. Sperling laughed. "He takes himself seriously enough for the both of us. Now tell me, dear, how long have you been in town? How do you like it? Where have you come from? Do you have an address for your grandparents? I'd like to write them."

Hannah laughed. Obviously Jake's mother didn't fear him, but then being his mother would most certainly affect the dynamics.

"I don't have the rooms ready. If you'll excuse me, I'd better take care of them."

Mrs. Sperling trotted after Hannah. "I'll help you."

Hannah stopped and faced the woman, her expression suitably serious even though her insides bubbled with amusement. "But I thought you were exhausted."

The older woman chuckled. "I've just experienced a miraculous recovery."

Hannah laughed with her. "I don't imagine anyone but you could get away with that."

Mrs. Sperling's brown eyes twinkled. "Get away with what?" Side by side, they climbed the stairs.

"I'd guess Jake expects his orders to be followed."

"He prefers it, I'm sure."

Hannah understood what wasn't said. Jake liked to be obeyed. Only his mother got away with defying him.

two

Jake reined his horse into the street, automatically touching the brim of his hat at several ladies, his thoughts still on his mother. He should have insisted she remain on the ranch. These trips to town were too strenuous for her. Miss Williams failed to realize it or she wouldn't have allowed his mother to talk her into offering them rooms in her damaged hotel. He should take his mother home immediately, but first he had to find the cattle buyers and negotiate a fair price for his steers. He and the other ranchers had discussed this, decided on what they considered a reasonable price, and agreed to hold out together for it. If they stood unified, no buyer could persuade one of them to undersell the others.

He stopped in front of one of the hotels and thudded across the sidewalk and into the quiet, clean-smelling interior to ask for the buyers and was informed that none of them had registered. He spun out and rode to the next hotel to receive the same response as he did at the third and last hotel in town. He paused to look around the lobby. Muted red carpet patterned with medallions, heavy maroon drapes—a calm, restful atmosphere. If they had to stay in town, why couldn't his mother have chosen one of these hotels?

Jake suddenly remembered his mother's request and headed for the livery. At the same time, he'd go by the station to see if the buyers had sent a telegram.

"Silas," he called as he stepped into the cool interior. "Is there a telegram for me?"

"No sir. I'd've found you if there was."

"You're sure Mr. Arnold hasn't sent a message?" Mr. Arnold was the one buyer Jake could count on. He'd been eager to do business with Jake and the others.

"Nothin'. Nothin' at all."

"Then they must be on their way." He'd have to cool his heels until they showed up. Easier said than done. He needed to finish his business and get back to the ranch. Even with Frank in charge, he couldn't neglect his responsibilities for long and expect things to hang together.

He then went to the livery. He spoke to one of the men working there. "Have my mother's things sent to the Sunshine Hotel." He tossed the man a handful of coins.

The worker gaped. "The Sunshine? But it's—"

Jake didn't allow him to finish. "Right away. She's waiting for them." He returned to his horse and rode to the pens to check on his herd.

Shorty patrolled on the left. On the other side, Jimbo's horse stood at the fence, but there was no sign of the boy. He'd been warned about keeping his mind on business.

Jake reined his horse to the right and edged around the fence. Jimbo sat on the edge of the wooden trough, his arm around a young girl. "Jimbo," Jake roared, "I don't pay you to socialize."

The boy jerked to his feet, his mouth working. The girl ducked behind him, her eyes wide as a cornered deer's.

"I've warned you—"

"Mr. Sperling, I ain't been visiting more'n a minute." The boy's Adam's apple bobbled as he swallowed hard. "This here's my sister, May." He swallowed noisily again. "I ain't seen her in three months. She's been telling me about Ma and Pa and the young ones."

Jake hesitated. By rights the boy had used up all his chances. It seemed a lifetime ago, but Jake remembered what it was like to be so young and uncertain, trying to deal with adult responsibilities and wondering if he could handle them successfully. "Find Con to take your place; then go visit your folks."

Jimbo threw himself on the back of his horse, pulled his sister after him, and headed for the road. "Thank you, Mr. Sperling," he called over his shoulder.

Jake watched the herd as he waited for Con to arrive. His thoughts turned toward the business he hoped to conduct. This delay was costly, as Mr. Arnold should know. Jake lounged on his horse, watching the animals shuffle about and settle into the new place. They'd be fine as long as nothing spooked them. But if Arnold didn't show up soon, he'd have the task of feeding and watering the bunch. He sighed. He wanted nothing more than to get back to the ranch where things were more predictable, more under his control. He did not like the feeling that he held on to the whole affair by a slippery rope.

Trying to keep his mother safe was more than enough challenge. He knew what she would do in town—shop until she exhausted herself. And without a dining room, she'd be forced to go out after a tiring day in order to eat. He would have to watch her carefully to ensure she didn't jeopardize her health before he got her back home.

As he often did when he was alone with his thoughts, he turned to prayer. It seemed more natural to talk to God on the back of a good horse than in church. *God, You know how*

I need to get these animals sold so I can get back to the ranch. It was up to him to see the ranch and the family properly taken care of, but he couldn't manage without God's help. He let the peace of knowing God's care sift through his tense thoughts then ended as he always did. *Help me fulfill my responsibilities.*

He shifted in the saddle as Con rode up to him. Jake gave him instructions on watching the herd but didn't hurry away. This was about the only place in the whole town where he felt comfortable. Finally, with a belly-cleansing sigh, he turned away. Time to deal with his mother and her needs.

He tied his horse in front of the hotel, crossed the sidewalk, and flicked a finger at the closed sign. Trust his mother to ignore the sign and the impracticality of staying here. But he feared if he insisted on moving, she'd upset herself and end up in bed. He sighed. Somehow they'd manage, inconvenient as it was.

He threw open the door and wrinkled his nose at the odor of smoke and lye. He'd sooner sleep with the cows. He heard angry muttering and followed the sound to the dining room. Hannah teetered on the top of a ladder struggling with blackened drapes. What was the woman thinking? Someone should tell her how dangerous ladders were.

"Miss, get down before you fall." His voice rang with the same tone he used with his hired hands, expecting them to jump and obey.

She jumped all right, and put herself completely off balance.

He leaped forward. "Stay right there," he ordered, shifting course to avoid the hole in the middle of the floor.

She pawed at the curtains, trying to right herself. A tear started at the edge where the material had burned. The sound began slow, like a beginning thought, then picked up speed. Her fragile balance shifted as the drapes parted company with the rod. Caught in the drape, she tumbled off the ladder.

In his haste to reach her, he stumbled over a chair and caught one foot between the rungs. He reached for her. In a tangle of charred drapes and a now broken wooden chair, they hit the floor. *Whoofs* of air exploded from two sets of lungs.

Jake couldn't move. His feet were snarled in chairs and fabric. The ladder had fallen across his legs. He'd have matching bruises to prove it.

Miss Williams sprawled across his chest, trying to fight her way out of the drapes encasing her. Her struggles landed elbows in his chest and face.

"Stop it," he muttered, and when she grew more frantic, he wrapped his arms around her, making it impossible for her to move.

"Let me up. I can't breathe." Her voice was muffled.

"Take it easy. I'll get you out." He kicked away the ladder and chair and rolled to his knees, then set to work untangling the fabric until she emerged.

She inhaled sharply and pushed hair out of her face, smearing charcoal over her cheeks, and shuddered. "That was dreadful. They stink."

He sucked in air filthy with the odor of the burned drapes as he pushed to his feet, feeling a pain in his shins from the encounter with the ladder. He dusted himself off. "You had no business up there. Who's in charge around here? How can he be so irresponsible as to allow you to do such a dangerous job? Where is he? I'll speak to him."

She scrambled from the drapes and stood up to face him,

her eyes boring into him. Very pretty hazel eyes, he noticed. "I am in charge. I am responsible for me. I don't need someone to take care of me."

"You can't be in charge."

"And why is that, Mr. Sperling?" Her voice was low, gentle. But her flashing eyes told the truth. She did not welcome his opinion.

Not that he cared what she thought. Someone had to see that she didn't do such foolish things in the future. And when had he gone from being "Jake" to "Mr. Sperling"? "This is not a job for a woman."

She pulled herself as tall as she could. Her eyes turned almost green; her cheeks flushed. "Really? And what do you propose to do about the fact that I own this place and intend to fix it up so I can open for guests?"

He struggled between anger at her stubbornness in refusing to give in to his hard stare and amusement at her attempt to be fierce. She'd find out soon enough there were things a woman had best leave for a man to do. It scraped his nerves to think she'd probably get hurt trying. His father had drilled into Jake that women were the weaker sex and men were responsible for protecting them. "You would have been injured if I hadn't caught you."

She flicked the idea away with a dismissive wave of her hand. "I was perfectly safe until you scared me. Don't you know you shouldn't sneak up on people like that?"

He narrowed his eyes. "Don't you know you shouldn't stand on the top of a ladder?" What was wrong with her? Didn't she care she might be injured? "In the future, stay on the ground."

"I don't see that my future is any of your business." She

spat the words out. Suddenly, her mouth rounded. "Oh, you're hurt." She reached for his cheek then pulled her hand back and pointed.

He touched the spot she indicated and saw blood on his fingers. "It's nothing."

"It needs to be tended to." She waved him toward a chair, saw it was charred, and waved him toward another. "I'll get something to clean it with." Without giving him a chance to protest, she hurried into the back room, which appeared to be the kitchen.

He chuckled when he heard her startled exclamation. She must have seen her reflection.

When she returned, her face and hair had been fixed. She approached him with a white cloth and a small basin of water. She put the basin on the table then hesitated.

"I can do it myself," he said.

She nodded and handed him the cloth.

He sponged at the area.

"A little more this way," she indicated. "It's still bleeding some."

The outer door opened. They both turned toward the sound.

His mother called.

"In here," he said.

His mother appeared in the doorway, took one look at him, and pressed her hand to her chest. "What happened?" She swayed.

"Mrs. Sperling." Hannah raced to his mother's side, but he tossed chairs out of his way and got there first. He swept his mother into his arms and headed for the sofa, Hannah hot on his heels.

"She should be at home," he muttered. "These trips to town are too strenuous for her."

As he laid her down, her eyes fluttered. She let out a little squeak. "You're bleeding."

"It's just a scratch." He rubbed her wrists and felt her pulse. It seemed strong enough.

"What were you doing?" his mother demanded.

Hannah spoke. "I'm afraid I'm responsible for any damage he's incurred. I decided I couldn't wait any longer for Mort to take down the burned drapes. But they decided to take me down instead. Your son broke my fall."

Mrs. Sperling pulled herself into a sitting position and glanced past her son to Hannah. "You aren't injured, too, are you?"

The girl moved closer. "Of course not. I'm pretty hardy." She glanced at Jake.

Jake was about to say he was hardy, too, when his mother answered for him. "He wrestles cows. I doubt you could hurt him much." She took Hannah's hand. "Rose's Ladies' Wear has the prettiest selection of bonnets. They've just arrived, Miss Rose said. You'll have to come with me to see them."

Feeling dismissed, Jake sat on one of the narrowed-backed, fancy-cushioned chairs.

"Mrs. Sperling, I couldn't possibly. I have to get this place ready for guests."

"But we are guests."

"Yes, my very first."

Jake's stomach growled loudly, announcing to everyone in the room he hadn't eaten since breakfast many hours ago.

Mother swung her feet to the floor. "I'm hungry, too. Shall we find supper?"

Jake eyed her. She seemed just a little pale and in no hurry to stand. He guessed she was still a little weak from her faint, though she'd probably deny it. "Mother, I don't think you're up to going out again."

His mother shot him an annoyed look. "I'm fine."

"You stay here, and I'll bring back something."

"I'd worry about you." She rubbed her chest as if it hurt.

Jake's stomach growled again. Louder. More persistent. He really needed to find food soon. But Mother looked so worried he didn't dare leave her. She leaned her head back, her eyelids fluttering.

"Hannah, perhaps you would be so kind as to prepare us something," Mother said.

The girl stared. "The dining room isn't open."

Mother lifted a weary hand. "I know that, my dear. But surely you eat. Wouldn't it be possible for us to share your meal?"

"B–but—," Hannah sputtered.

Jake knew he should have put his foot down from the first. This was not a safe place for his mother. The dining room was in shambles. Hannah seemed bent on risking life and limb to prove she could do a job beyond her capabilities. "Mother, you can't be serious. You knew when you insisted on staying here that we'd have to go out to eat."

She pressed her hand to her left shoulder. "I know, but it's not like we need anything special."

She spoke for herself. Jake was about ready to butcher one of his own steers and roast it in the alley. He got to his feet and headed for the door. "Anything in particular you'd like me to bring back?"

His mother moaned and fell back on the cushion. He

halted. Dare he leave her?

"I don't mind sharing my supper with you." Hannah spoke softly, sending Jake a look that dared him to argue.

"That would be lovely," Mother whispered without opening her eyes.

Jake ached to reject Hannah's offer. His mouth flooded at the promise of a thick steak. But his mother's fragile state swayed him against his personal wants. With a sigh, he mentally kissed the steak good-bye. He jerked a chair to his mother's side and plunked down on it. "That will be fine," he told Hannah.

"I'll get right at it." She spun on her heels and headed for the kitchen.

Jake watched his mother, worried she was so quiet. He made up his mind. "In the morning I'll hire someone to take you home."

Her eyes opened quickly, and she fixed him with a determined look. "You'll do no such thing. I have shopping to do."

"You'll exhaust yourself."

"How can you think of sending me home as though I've been naughty?"

Jake felt caught between wanting to obey his mother and being the one responsible for her health.

His mother draped her arm over her forehead. She looked so exhausted, he decided he would personally take her home as soon as it was light out.

"Don't deprive me of this little pleasure," she pleaded.

He wanted to say no. But he couldn't. After all, she must get lonely at the ranch. "Very well, if you promise to be careful."

"I promise." She smiled gratefully. "Now why don't you go

see if you can help that sweet girl?"

"Me?" Give him a fire and a slab of beef, and he could cook up a meal to satisfy the largest appetite, but he turned all feet and thumbs when he tried to do things indoors.

"I'd help, but—," his mother began.

"You stay here and rest." He reluctantly planted his feet under him and made for the dining room door, certain the last thing Hannah needed was his assistance. He stuck his nose into the room where she worked. "How can I help?" Should he warn her of his ineptitude in the kitchen?

She stopped chopping something into a bowl of flour and considered him. "Help?" She sounded so surprised, he stepped into the room.

"I'm sure there's something I can do."

She looked about ready to refuse.

"I insist." Mother would have a fit if he didn't do something.

Hannah didn't look very happy about it, but she nodded. "Very well. You can slice the chicken." She wiped her hands on her apron and pulled a glass platter from the cupboard. "Arrange it on this."

He held the platter gingerly. It shone in the light and looked like it would break if he held it too hard. Or worse, slip from his fingers and shatter on the floor if he didn't trap it firmly. Not daring to breathe, he marched around to the opposite end of the long wooden table. Very carefully, he put the platter next to the jar of canned chicken. He tested the lid, found she'd already loosened it, and grabbed a fork she shoved toward him.

Now he had to get the pieces of chicken out of the tightly packed jar. How hard could it be? Nothing compared to dropping a lasso over a racing cow. He clenched the jar firmly in one hand, stabbed the fork into the contents, and yanked hard. He practically jerked the jar out of his fist but didn't remove any meat. He put the jar squarely back on the table. He thought of wrestling it to the ground, using brute force and ignorance on it.

"Wiggle the meat out of the top," Hannah said.

He stole a glance at her, suspecting she found this amusing. But she seemed engrossed in rolling out some dough on the tabletop. If he didn't miss his guess, they were having biscuits—with chicken, if he could manage the simple task.

He tightened his grip on the jar and sawed the meat back and forth until it slipped through the top and promptly flew across the table to plop in front of Hannah.

"Whoops," she said and waited for him to retrieve it.

He grabbed it with the fork and pinned it to the platter, where he butchered it with a knife. Slices. . .she wouldn't be getting. Chunks would have to do.

He managed to get the rest of the chicken from the jar to the platter without any disaster. Then he backed away, hoping to escape.

"The biscuits will be a few minutes. Where do you want to eat?"

"Obviously the dining room is out."

"Obviously."

He glanced around the kitchen, guessing Hannah ate alone here most nights. It was a cozy place with the range at one end, a big window at the other, and well-stocked cupboards in between. He was about to suggest this would be a nice place to eat when she spoke.

"Perhaps I should move one of the tables into the lobby." She headed for the dining room.

"Table in the lobby would be fine." She didn't need his consent, but it would be nice to be consulted. After all it was he and his mother who were being served.

She chose a table in the far corner, one hardly affected by the fire, and started to push it toward the door.

He grabbed it.

"Thank you," she said, all prim and formal.

"You're welcome," he replied, equally formal.

"I'll get some hot water and scrub it."

"I'll get some chairs," he said.

"I can manage on my own."

"So you've said, but what kind of man would I be if I sat and watched you lug furniture around?"

They hurried to the doorway. Arrived at the same time.

He stood back and nodded for her to go first. "Please."

She nodded and preceded him. "Thank you."

"You're welcome."

His mother groaned. "Can we manage without the stiff politeness? It's a little tiresome."

"I'd be glad to," Jake said, "if Hannah will stop saying thank you every time I move."

Hannah opened her mouth as if to argue then shrugged. "I wouldn't want to be tiresome." She hurried to the kitchen for hot water.

He sighed. She'd been so warm and friendly down at the rail yards. But now she acted like he was personally responsible for the fire in her hotel. Why the big switch? He'd done nothing to make her so disagreeable. Unless. . . He thought of her reaction when he'd told her to stay off the ladder. Maybe she blamed him for the torn drapes. But that didn't make sense. She only planned to dispose of them.

Slowly a thought surfaced. Had he offended her by telling her she couldn't run this place on her own? But she couldn't. Didn't take a Philadelphia education to realize that. He grabbed two chairs and placed them next to the table.

Hannah returned, scrubbed the chairs and table, spread a snow-white tablecloth, and then set the table.

His mother sat up. "Where's the other chair?"

"What other chair?" Jake demanded.

"Do you expect Hannah to serve us after she's offered to share her meal? Get another chair so she can eat with us."

Hannah backed away. "Oh no, Mrs. Sperling. Really. I prefer to take care of you first." She fled to the kitchen.

"Jake, how could you?" his mother whispered. "Persuade her to join us."

He snagged a chair and put it at the table, then went to find Hannah. She didn't look up when he entered the room. "Please join us for supper."

She glanced up then, staring at him long and hard.

"I insist," he added for good measure.

"Very well. You're the boss. Please make yourself comfortable. I'll bring in the food."

He wanted to explain it wasn't because he was the boss. Nor even because his mother had wanted it. He had unnecessarily offended her by setting out only two chairs. He hadn't meant to. But he didn't know how to make up for it. It seemed everything he did only made matters worse. He returned to the other room. "She'll be joining us in a few minutes," he informed his mother as he assisted her to the table.

Hannah arrived with a huge tray balanced on one hand. He might have offered to help but decided it was safer for everyone if he sat tight. Hot biscuits, a platter of chicken that looked nothing like the mess he'd created, a tray of cheese, and a pot of blackberry jam made his stomach lurch in expectation.

"This is lovely, dear," his mother said. "How did you manage it in such a short time?"

Hannah smiled. "My grandmother left a well-stocked pantry."

At least she got along with his mother. He wondered who would ask the blessing.

Mother solved the problem. "Hannah, would you like Jake to pray over the food?"

Hannah looked hard at Jake. Did he see surprise? Guardedness? As if she expected him to be a pagan just because he'd inadvertently offended her? Though, in fact, he'd been nothing but kind and accommodating. He'd even agreed to stay in her derelict hotel. How was that for kind? And he'd been helpful. He glanced at the platter of chicken that she'd rearranged. Well, he'd tried.

"Please, Mr. Sperling, would you?"

He pulled his attention back to her request. "Jake. It's Jake. Remember?" She'd been a lot less formal when he'd shown her around the cattle. He corralled his wandering thoughts and bowed his head to murmur a quick prayer.

After the prayer, Hannah passed the food. "I hope the next time you're in town I'll be officially reopened."

Jake slathered butter on the biscuit and took a bite. "The repairs seem like an extraordinarily big task for a woman on her own. Seems they'd best be dealt with by a man. Or better yet, a crew of hardy men."

Hannah ducked her head, contemplated her food for a moment, and then shot him a look flashing with annoyance. She obviously did not like him pointing out the impossibility of a woman dealing with this job. "I'm quite capable of handling it. My father raised me to take care of myself, and I would never disappoint him by backing out of a challenge."

"Does he know the hotel has been gutted by fire?"

"He's gone."

"Gone?"

His mother sighed. "Jake, don't be so thick. She means he's passed away. I'm sorry, dear. I can see how much you miss him. Now, let's talk about something else." She pinned Jake with a glance. "Jake, another topic, please."

"Like what, Mother? The cows?"

"Really, Jake, that isn't all you know."

She was wrong. What did he know besides cows, ranching, and work?

But his mother persisted. "You could ask her about herself."

Jake studied his mother. She smiled.

"Very well." Jake turned to Hannah. "Tell me about yourself."

Sweetly, she said, "What would you like to know?"

"I think you are enjoying my discomfort."

"But no, sir. Why would you think such a thing?"

"Maybe because of that little smile teasing the corners of your mouth."

Her smile widened. Her eyes sparkled with mischief. Something inside him jerked like a cow reaching the end of a rope. It left him breathless and dizzy.

Suddenly he was curious about her. What did she like to do? How did she spend her free time? Did she have free time? He had his doubts. This hotel needed a ton of work. "Is your mother alive?"

"Yes. Alive and well and living with her new husband back

East." She ducked her head, ate a bite, and then looked at him. "What about you? Where's your father?"

"My father is also dead." He heard his mother's indrawn breath and patted her hand.

"Things have never been the same since he passed on," his mother said.

"I've tried to continue his work." It seemed he could never live up to his father's ideals.

"That's not what I mean. You've done a very good job, my dear. I just never expected to have to grow old alone."

He laughed. "Alone? You have a cook who is also a dear friend. Audrey and the boys are in and out so often I'm surprised they don't claim bedrooms. And then there's me. We share the same house. When are you ever alone?"

"It's not the same."

He relented. "I understand what you mean."

Hannah watched the exchange and smiled. "Tell me about the ranch."

He settled back, comfortable with this topic. He talked about how his father had decided money was in cows, not gold, and picked a spot with lots of water and grass and protection. "He had a dream for Quinten to become the cattle capital of the West. And when the railway came, he was ready." He realized how long he'd been talking about the ranch and skidded to a halt.

She smiled. "It sounds fascinating. I've always lived in the city. Father owned a successful mercantile store until his death. I always think of him smelling like old cheese and kerosene." Her smile faltered for a moment. "My stepfather is a banker. My grandparents are the only adventuresome members of the family."

"Until now," Jake said. "Seems to me you've acquired a man-sized adventure here. It looks like a ton of work."

"I'd say it appears considerably easier than trying to corral a herd of wild cows."

They all laughed, though Jake's amusement was tempered by annoyance. Chasing cows was men doing men's work. Hannah's trying to fix up this place on her own didn't make a lick of sense.

⋙

Hannah toyed with her napkin. She would have enjoyed company—a pleasant change from eating alone or trying to converse with Mort—if it had been only Mrs. Sperling. But Jake robbed her of that enjoyment. He didn't approve of her independence. Like Otto, he wanted her to conform to "acceptable" behavior, which meant being a docile woman who knew her place. No managing without a man's input and help.

She ducked her head so no one would see her smile. Jake's help in the kitchen was laughable. Of course, like Otto, he'd probably willingly admit the kitchen was a woman's domain. Hannah had no wish to become a man. Certainly no hankering to chase cows just to prove she could do a man's work. She wanted only the freedom to make choices, express her opinions, and follow her dreams.

She knew not all people longed for independence the way she did, but God had given her the desire and now the opportunity. She'd not let criticism or adversity deter her.

The door opened and two men strode in. She sighed. Either the whole town was illiterate or thought closed signs didn't apply to them. The men wore big cowboy hats they quickly took off. "Mrs. Sperling," each said.

"Mr. Riggs and Mr. Martin," Mrs. Sperling said. "Meet Miss Williams, new owner of the Sunshine Hotel."

"Miss." They nodded toward her then turned their attention to Jake. "Our herds are a mile from town. Thought the buyers could come out there and see them."

Jake pushed back from the table and rose to his feet. "None of them has showed yet."

"They ain't here?" The shorter one, Mr. Martin, looked angry.

"There's a train due in twenty minutes," Jake said. "Let's go meet them." He tossed some coins on the table. "Mother, while I'm out, try to get your rest."

Hannah's cheeks burned. She hadn't expected to be paid for sharing her meager meal with them. It had been a courtesy, but he'd effectively put her in her place. Or rather, the place he expected of her—a willing servant to his demands.

She grabbed the coins and hurried after him. "I don't want—" But the door closed behind him, and by the time she threw it open, he was riding away. She stared after him, her insides coiling like the fire-damaged curls of wallpaper. She sucked in several deep breaths before she returned to the table.

"My dear." The older woman patted her hand. "He didn't mean to insult you. He's just very single-minded about business. He takes his responsibilities so seriously." She sighed. "He was only fifteen when my husband was injured in an accident. Seth barely survived. He never walked again. Never got out of bed even. Although I miss him so much, it was a mercy when he went. No more pain and suffering. I picture him in heaven, enjoying the use of his legs again." She sniffled into a hankie.

Hannah murmured her condolences, but when she began to clear the table, Mrs. Sperling caught her hand.

"Do you mind listening to an old woman's prattle?"

Hannah laughed. "You aren't old nor do you prattle." She sensed the woman longed for someone to converse with. Hannah wasn't opposed to the idea. It had been lonely with only Mort or passersby to talk to. Work could wait. "I'd love to sit and chat."

Mrs. Sperling picked up where she left off. "Seth couldn't move about, but he still ran the place. Jake became his legs and hands. He expected a lot from the boy. And now Jake expects even more from himself."

Hannah didn't want to hear about Jake. She especially did not want to listen to his mother excuse his behavior. "You have a daughter?"

The woman smiled with pride. "Audrey. She's the opposite of Jake in many ways. Never worries about responsibility. She knows how to enjoy life. She married Harvey, who owns the neighboring ranch."

"You're very proud of her."

"I'm proud of both of them."

Hannah knew Mrs. Sperling believed her words, but when she spoke about Audrey, her voice held a whole different sound than when she spoke of Jake—as if Audrey pleased her and Jake served her. Hannah dismissed the idea. She was reading more into it than she had any right. She knew nothing about the family.

She let Mrs. Sperling talk for a long time and served her tea and cookies as they visited. But after the woman tried several times to unsuccessfully hide her yawns, Hannah stood. "I think I'd better take care of these dishes."

"And I'd better go to my room. Thank you again for sharing your meal with us."

Hannah cleaned up the meal, tidied the kitchen, and hauled the drapes out to the alley where Mort could finish burning them in the morning. She yawned and stretched. She would like to go to bed, but until Jake returned, she couldn't lock the front door. She had no choice but to wait up.

She went to her room, picked up her Bible, and returned to the lobby to settle herself behind the desk and wait. She opened the scriptures where she had placed the bookmark last night—Deuteronomy, one of her favorite books. She began to read, enjoying the retelling of the desert journey and how God had worked among people. It encouraged her to know He still did.

Her head jerked as sleep overcame her. How long did Jake intend to stay out? She pushed to her weary feet, shivering as someone thudded past on the street. She'd never stayed open so late. She felt alone and vulnerable. If one of the cowboys with too much drink in him came through the door. . .

She made up her mind then and there and hurried out to the small building in the back to knock on Mort's door. A light shone from inside, so she guessed she wouldn't be waking him.

He opened up. "Yes, miss."

"I need you to watch the desk. Mr. Sperling is still out."

He nodded. "I'll be right there."

She hurried back inside. Thankfully, Mort had not grumbled.

❧

At the station the next morning, Jake climbed off his horse and momentarily leaned against its warm flank. No cattle buyers had come in on last night's train. Jake managed to snag a few hours of restless sleep; then he, Riggs, and Martin met the first train this morning. Still no buyers.

Riggs stared at the train as it pulled from the station. "Where are they?"

Jake's gut convulsed. "Let's find out."

The men strode three abreast into the depot.

The stationmaster glanced up at their approach and looked worried. Jake spoke for them all. "Silas, is there a telegram for me?"

"No sir, Mr. Sperling." He glanced at the telegraph key. "Nothin' at all."

"Then I want to send a message," Jake said, his voice as hard as the knot in his stomach. "Mr. Arnold. Stop. Where are you? Stop. Why the delay? Stop."

Riggs nudged him. "Forget 'where are you.' We just want to know why he's not here."

Jake nodded. "Take out that part."

Silas glanced at the three of them, waiting for them to nod. "Send it," Jake said. "And the man better have a good reason for being so late. I'll accept nothing short of a death in his family."

Martin smacked his fist into his palm. "Or serious injury."

Jake knew what he meant. Martin was known to have a short fuse. He wouldn't be opposed to using his fists if Mr. Arnold was simply dangling them at the end of a rope hoping to force them to sell at a lower price. "Best wait and hear what he has to say for himself. Could be he's on his way right now."

They turned and strode toward the door. The men parted ways outside. Riggs and Martin headed back to their herds.

Jake returned to the hotel, where he lingered a moment at his horse's side. Things just couldn't get any worse. As he thumped up the wooden steps, he thought he heard a familiar sound and shuddered. He was tired. His mind played tricks. At least he hoped so.

But as he opened the door, he realized things were about to get a whole lot worse.

three

"Uncle Jake. Uncle Jake." Two bodies launched themselves at him. They were small. Together they weighed less than a hardy calf, but he knew from experience that they had the ability to cut him down at the knees if he didn't brace himself. He backed up until he hit a solid wall and prepared for the attack. And just in time. One small body hit him at knee level. The other grabbed Jake's hands and crawled up his body like some kind of monkey.

"Hey, boys. Where did you come from?" Guess it was too much to expect Audrey would keep them at home and out of his hair.

The smallest one, the four-year-old knee nipper named Sammy, screamed, "We get to stay with Gamma."

Luke, a year older but only a few pounds heavier, continued to pull himself up Jake's body until he planted his face directly in front of Jake's. "Momma said we could have fun in town."

"She did, did she?" He shuddered, picturing just what sort of fun the pair would have.

"Where's your mother? Where's Grandma?" He edged his face past Luke's and located his mother sitting next to the window in the lobby. "Where's Audrey?"

"She wanted to go with Harvey on his business trip. She asked if I would mind keeping the boys. Of course I agreed."

"You can't keep them here."

"Why not? They'll enjoy a few days in town."

"A few days?" He sputtered and stopped to rope in his thoughts. "We can't keep them out of trouble on the ranch. On two ranches. How do you expect to corral them in town?"

He looked around the lobby, seeing it for the first time. The prissy furniture. The breakable knickknacks. The polished wooden floor—beautiful and just perfect for two little boys to slide on, leaving scratches he guessed Hannah wouldn't appreciate.

His mother answered his question. "You can herd two hundred head of cows by yourself. Surely you can keep an eye on two little boys."

"Me?" When had he volunteered for the job? "Can't you keep them here?" As he finished studying his surroundings, his doubts multiplied.

Hannah came to the door of the dining room, an adoring expression on her face as she watched the boys.

"Don't let their innocent appearance fool you," he warned her. "This pair can be deadly."

She tore her gaze from Sammy, her smile receding as she met Jake's eyes. "They're sweet."

He glanced past her to the dining room, visions of one of the youngsters falling into the hole, and saw she'd erected a barrier with lengths of wood. He knew it wouldn't keep the boys out. Nothing but a solid wall would.

Luke squirmed out of his arm, and as Jake tried to snag him, Sammy escaped. The pair circled the room, screaming at the top of their lungs. His mother closed her eyes and pressed her lips together so hard they disappeared. He could hardly blame her. The racket was worse than weaning time at the ranch. *Ahh*, for the peace of his cows. . . He could think of nothing he'd sooner do than get on his horse and head out of town.

"Have they eaten?" He was forced to raise his voice to make himself heard.

Hannah chuckled. "Steadily since they came."

He groaned, remembering their bottomless appetites. He grabbed Sammy as he roared past. "How would you like to go get something to eat?"

Jake winced as the boy roared his approval. "You don't have to yell. I'm not deaf." Though he would be if Sammy kept screaming in his ear.

"I like yelling," the boy said.

"Yeah, I noticed." He turned to the other screaming child. "Luke, if you stop running and yelling, I'll take you to the restaurant."

Luke skidded to a halt. "Can I have anything I want?"

"I suppose so."

Luke screamed his approval and raced for the door. Sammy slipped from Jake's grasp and galloped after him, doubling the noise.

"Halt!" Jake yelled. But neither boy slowed down. Jake almost fell as he skidded to the door in time to stop Sammy but too late to corral Luke who stood on the sidewalk still screaming. Jake's horse reared, and a rider on the street struggled to keep from being thrown into the dirt.

Jake grabbed Luke and yanked him inside. "Stop that racket right now."

"What?" the boy yelled.

"Stop yelling!" Jake realized he was yelling now and pressed the heel of his hand to his forehead. "Please, be quiet." Blessed silence filled the room. "That's better. Mother, shall we go to the restaurant now?"

His mother fluttered her fingers. "I have a headache. You go without me."

He stared at her. "Me? Take these two out by myself?" He shook his head hard.

"Jake, there are only two of them."

"And one of me." He shifted his gaze to Hannah. If she came along there would be two for two.

She must have read his thoughts. She held up a cloth. "I'm working."

"But you have to eat, don't you?"

She crossed her arms and looked disinterested in his plight. He tried to think of a way to convince her. If she were one of his outfit, how would he handle it? Ask nicely? And then insist. She wasn't one of the hired hands, but surely the same process would work for her.

"Hannah, I would appreciate it if you would accompany us to lunch."

She glanced over her shoulder as if measuring the work she had.

"You aren't going to finish up anytime soon, so why not take a break?"

She shifted her gaze from the dining room to the two boys.

He wasn't above using the pair as bait. "Boys, wouldn't you like Miss Hannah to come with us?"

He grimaced as they yelled, "Yes!" Why did his sister let them be so loud?

Hannah smiled at their eagerness. "Very well. I'll come along. Give me a minute to clean up."

Jake had been about to say she didn't need to bother. They weren't going anyplace fancy. Not with his two nephews. Where he planned to go there would be working men and cowboys. Besides, she looked perfectly presentable in her pretty little blue cotton dress, but she hurried away before he could get the words into shape to speak.

He tried to keep the boys at his side while they waited, but even though she was only gone a few minutes, by the time she returned, they were circling the room at full gallop, their voices about to shatter the windows. Jake captured Sammy as he raced by and wondered if he would have to hog-tie the pair to get them to the restaurant in one piece.

Hannah held out her hand. "Luke, walk with me." The boy trotted over and took her hand as simple as that. She glanced at each boy. "Now let's see who can be the quietest."

"For how long?" Sammy asked.

"Until we get back. I think I might have some cookies for anyone who is quiet the whole time we're gone. You can talk, but quietly. Like gentlemen."

Sammy squirmed to his feet and took Jake's hand.

Jake gave Hannah a hard look. "How did you do that?"

She shrugged. "I just asked them." She'd pulled her hair into a soft roll that made him notice her pretty features. A wide, smiling mouth, a pert little nose with just a hint of freckles, and hazel eyes that he already knew could turn cold one minute and fiery the next.

"I asked them, too. It didn't work as you might have noticed."

"You ordered them."

He blinked. "I—"

She smiled sweetly. "There's a difference."

"Of course. I know that." Except he couldn't remember ordering the boys about. And if she thought he had, then maybe he didn't know.

They strode down the street. The boys were so quiet, Jake

shuddered, wondering when they would explode. He glanced at Hannah. She smiled as if she enjoyed a secret. Suddenly he relaxed. This wasn't going to be so bad after all.

They reached the restaurant. Several of his outfit nodded greetings and watched, as curious as newborn calves, as Jake found a table for his group next to the window. He and Luke sat across from Hannah and Sammy. Hannah fussed about Sammy for a moment then left him to down the glass of water the waitress brought. Beside him, Luke did the same. Jake tensed, ready to rescue a glass should either boy upset his.

They drained their water and sat on the edge of their chairs swinging their feet. Sammy screamed as they kicked each other.

Jake thumped the tabletop. "Boys, keep the noise down."

Hannah shot him a look that made him squirm more than his words had made either boy squirm. She touched Sammy's shoulder. "Remember, speak quietly if you want cookies when we get back."

Sammy stopped pumping his legs. "What kind?"

"What's your favorite?" she asked.

He glanced at Luke. "What is?" he whispered.

Luke whispered back, "Molasses."

Sammy turned toward Hannah, serious as a judge. "Molasses."

"Then it's a good thing that's what I baked this morning, isn't it?"

Jake studied Sammy. Light brown hair and blue eyes, like his father, and a rash of freckles. Luke, darker than Sammy, didn't have quite the innocent look Sammy managed to fool strangers with but was just as capable of mischief. Jake couldn't imagine how the pair got into so much trouble. It seemed to stick to them like a bad smell to a pair of boots.

Audrey had dressed them to come to town in dark brown trousers and matching pale brown shirts that made them look like innocent young children. In fact, if he didn't know them so well he might have been as fooled as Hannah, her eyes all warm as she watched them.

She looked healthy enough. Good bones. Good conformity. Good gait—though he supposed it was called something different in a woman. The sort of woman a man wanted to take home and care for. Why did she want to do a man's job? What would it prove except her foolishness at trying? And it would bring only disappointment—or worse, if she fell off a ladder with no one around to catch her.

The murmur of conversation and the clinking of china in the kitchen filled the silence as Sammy pressed his lips together so he would pass the quiet test.

The serving girl placed heaping plates before them. Jake grabbed Luke's hands before he could dig in. "Grace first." He murmured a quick prayer with one eye not quite shut so he could watch Sammy. He almost relaxed as Hannah covered the boy's hands with hers.

The food was robust, just like a man needed. For the first time he realized how few women were in the room. Probably most of them preferred one of the fancier places. Would Hannah? He'd seen her scrubbing walls and dragging down old drapes. She'd had flour dusting her nose as she bent over a table rolling out biscuits. He tried to imagine her in the finest restaurant in town and found not only could he, but he liked it. Right then and there, he promised himself he'd take her one day. For his enjoyment as much as hers. Though she had probably been to all of them already. Maybe accompanied by someone else. He was startled to realize how much he didn't like that idea.

"Have you been to the other restaurants in town?" he asked.

"Not yet. I've been rather preoccupied with the hotel."

"What made you think you—" He paused. Better not suggest she couldn't run the hotel. He'd already noticed she seemed a little sensitive about that. "What made you think you wanted to run a hotel?"

She laughed softly, a sound like the wind racing through the trees. "Actually I never thought of it until my grandparents asked me if I'd like to, and then I jumped at the opportunity."

"So this is a sudden decision?" If he intended to ask her to the fanciest restaurant in town, he'd better do it before she changed her mind about the hotel business and headed back East.

She reached over and cut Sammy's meat into little pieces. "Sudden? I suppose. Though I'd been praying for such an opportunity for a long time. I just hadn't known what shape it would take."

He worked that about in his head as he devoted some attention to his meal. He just couldn't see it the way she did. "How is it an opportunity for a young woman alone?"

She paused with a forkful of mashed potatoes halfway to her mouth. Her eyes flashed like sun off rocks lying below the surface of a mountain stream. All shiny and bright. "Perhaps it depends on the young woman."

Their gazes clashed. Locked. He read determination, stubbornness even, in her eyes. He sought the right words to express his feelings, not willing to concede to her opinion, wanting to save her from disappointment when she found she just couldn't do it on her own. Not wishing to say again what he really thought—that it was man's work she aimed to do—he settled on saying, "Everyone has his limit."

Her eyes held a glittering challenge. "What's yours, Jake Sperling?"

Jake's thoughts tangled like old rope, caught in things her eyes seemed to promise—knowing, sharing, longing, and hundreds of butterfly ideas he couldn't name. His mouth opened, but no words formed in his brain.

Luke's grunt pulled his attention away from her probing look to the child struggling with his meat. Jake reached over with his knife. "I'll cut it."

Luke shook his head. "I do it myself." He dug his fork in harder. The meat skidded away and landed in Jake's lap. He grabbed it and wiped in on the napkin before putting it back on Luke's plate and, ignoring the child's stubborn glower, cut it into pieces. Only then did he turn back to Hannah and answer her question. "Maybe my limit is little boys."

She laughed, and the sound sank into his senses like a breath of spring. "Little boys are becoming men. I'd think you, of all people, would encourage their independence."

"Independence means responsibility, and these two aren't ready for that." He felt the heat of her look—like being branded. He wondered what she thought. He waited for her to say it.

Someone jostled his elbow. "Hey, Jake. When are we heading back to the ranch?"

He turned to Zeke and saw several others hovered behind him. "Waiting for the buyers."

Zeke looked surprised. "Thought they was supposed to be here when we arrived."

Jake tried to shrug it off. "I expected them." He pushed back from the table. "Boys, I'll be in touch real soon." Luke and Sammy had cleaned their plates down to the pattern on the china. "Are you done?" he asked Hannah.

She nodded.

"Then let's be on our way." He had to take care of the herd.

&

Hannah fell into step beside him, liking the sound of his boots striking the wooden sidewalk. A good, solid sound that she hoped would force her thoughts back to a firm base.

Her reactions to this man were sharp and sometimes unexpected. Why should she care if he thought she couldn't run the hotel on her own? It didn't matter, except his attitude, so like Otto's, annoyed her half to death. And just when she'd decided the sooner he returned to his ranch the better as far as she was concerned, her opinion of him shifted. Watching him cut Luke's meat and seeing the way the little guys adored him made her insides feel like warm cream. Why it should be, she couldn't say. But she didn't like it. It made it hard for her to remember the importance of her independence.

She increased the length of her stride, trying to keep up with him.

The boys' voices rang out clear and strong as they galloped ahead like wild colts.

"Luke, Sammy, slow down," Jake ordered. The pair hesitated half a step then roared forward. Jake groaned. "Trouble just waiting to happen."

Hannah chuckled at his consternation. "You're proud of them, and I don't blame you. Sammy is almost pretty but definitely a boy full of sweet, innocent mischief. Luke is already learning to temper his natural bent for finding trouble."

Jake snorted. "I don't see the innocent part, but trouble is their middle name."

Hannah laughed breathlessly as she tried to keep up with Jake's long strides.

"I need to get back to my responsibilities," he said.

"Me, too. I've noticed nothing gets done when I'm away."

"What about Mort?"

"Yes, Mort." Did he think Mort made up for her trying to do a "man's work"? She would soon change his mind about that. And about her needing a man. She could manage on her own. "Mort has one speed—slightly faster than a crawl. In his mind, he also has one job—night clerk. I haven't much call for such a position right now. I've tried to get him to do a few other things. Mind you, I'm not complaining. I appreciate his help with the water and fires."

"He should do more. I'll speak to him."

"Our arrangement works just fine."

"I can't believe your stepfather allowed you to come out here alone."

She stopped and gave him a look full of hot displeasure. "My stepfather tried to make me reconsider. He tried to force me to become an obedient young woman who'd let him make all her decisions. But he has no right. Neither do you. My father encouraged me to be independent. I will not disappoint him." Ignoring the way his mouth dropped open then shut with a click, she steamed forward.

In three quick strides he caught up. "Hannah, no need to get angry."

She slowed her steps. "I'm not angry. No. That's not true. I am angry. I'm tired of you suggesting I should give up my hotel because I'm not a man."

"Well, you're not." He chuckled.

She was not amused. "I'm not trying to be. But that doesn't

mean I can't manage without one." She stopped and faced him. "Now, does it?" Her words were soft, yet he'd better not make the mistake of thinking she'd given in.

She watched emotions shift across his face—stubbornness as if he intended to argue, confusion as if the whole idea surprised him so much he didn't know how to tame it, and then quiet resignation. But if she thought he'd accepted her stand, he quickly corrected her.

"You'll find out soon enough that you can't manage on your own."

She clamped her mouth shut to keep from telling him exactly what she thought of his attitude. *Lord, forgive me for being so angry.* She took a deep breath and allowed peace to return to her heart. "Sorry, but I intend to prove you wrong."

He shook his head. His mouth pulled down at the corners.

Hannah couldn't tell if he was resigned to her decision or sad because he expected her to fail.

"If you change your mind and want some help—"

She cut him off. "I won't." She headed after the boys again.

"Boys, slow down," Jake called. Then quieter, for her benefit, he added, "They're getting awfully loud."

She saw Sammy's boot catch on a board and gasped as he sprawled headfirst into a display of buckets outside Johnson's Hardware Store. The buckets tipped over with a crash that rattled the air. She and Jake rushed forward together.

A horse whinnied. Hannah caught a glimpse of a rider trying to control his mount and noticed a flash as a wagon roared by with the driver sawing on the reins. But her attention centered on Sammy. Several buckets bounced off various parts of his body. She feared he'd be injured. She reached for the child. "Sammy."

He looked past her to his uncle. "Uncle Jake," he cried.

Jake swept the boy into his arms and sat down on the sidewalk to hold him close. Sammy wrapped his small arms around Jake's neck and hung on, sobbing loudly. For a minute, Jake hugged the boy so tight Hannah feared he'd do further damage, and then Jake eased him back and looked into his face. "Are you hurt?"

The boy screamed.

"Where?" Without waiting for an answer, Jake scrubbed his hands through the child's hair searching for damage. He pulled up the boy's shirt and checked for injuries. Satisfied he wasn't seriously hurt, Jake pulled Sammy back into his arms and held him tight. "You'll be fine, little guy."

Hannah's eyes stung with tears. Not from sympathy for Sammy's pain, even though she felt sorry for the boy. She wasn't even sure she could say exactly why she felt so close to crying except she envied the child that certainty of love and approval and acceptance from Jake. Her father had given her the same thing, and she missed it almost as much as she missed him.

Luke hung back, concern written all over his face. As soon as he saw his little brother was uninjured, he threw himself at Jake.

As Jake's arms opened, Hannah's heart unfurled around the edges like a springtime leaf opening to the warmth of the season.

Jake pushed to his feet and clasped a boy in each hand. "Time to get back to your grandmother."

Sammy practically beat the door down as they arrived at the hotel and screamed for his "Gamma."

"Nothing wrong with his lungs," Jake murmured.

Hannah grinned as Mrs. Sperling captured Sammy in a

hug and tried to piece together the story spilling from the two boys. "I'm just glad he wasn't hurt."

Hannah left the family to fill in the details and headed for the kitchen. She really did have to get to work. Before she reached the dining room, the outer door burst open and a young man skidded to stop and glanced around. "Mr. Sperling," he shouted, "got a telegram for you."

Jake took the yellow paper and glanced at the message. With a muffled complaint, he crumpled it in his fist. "Someone had better have a good explanation for this."

"You need me for anything else?" the boy asked.

Jake gave him some coins and dismissed him.

"What is it?" Mrs. Sperling demanded.

Jake hesitated. "Nothing for you to worry about, Mother."

"If it's to do with the ranch, it concerns me." She held out her hand. "I want to see it."

Hannah grinned at Jake's helpless expression. Mrs. Sperling certainly bounced from fluttering, helpless female to strong woman when it suited her.

But Jake didn't relinquish the telegram. "It's from Mr. Arnold saying the buyers aren't coming."

"Does he say why?" the older woman asked.

Again Jake hesitated, and Hannah sensed the message said more than he cared to share with his mother.

"Jake, you might as well tell me. I can deal with the facts better than whatever my imagination dredges up."

"He says he's received information our animals are diseased." He bunched his hands into fists. "I'll find out who started this rumor, and when I do. . ."

A shiver raced across Hannah's shoulders. She felt pity for the person causing his anger. Jake would deal with him severely.

The Dreams of Hannah Williams 57

Jake was not a man to thwart. He expected compliance with his orders. She wondered if that extended to young women who challenged him about running a hotel.

The two ranchers she'd met the day before stomped into the lobby. "Saw Silas's boy over here. Did you hear something from the buyers?" Riggs demanded.

Jake handed him the telegram.

Martin read it over his shoulder. "It's Murphy. No doubt about it."

Hannah watched Sammy's eyes grow wide as Martin swung his fist as if pummeling the man named Murphy.

Jake held up his hand to silence the other two. "Mother, would you take the boys upstairs or outside?"

Mrs. Sperling had already risen. "I think we'll go see if we can find some penny candy."

Hannah squatted to the boys' level as they passed. "I haven't forgotten the cookies. I'll save them for when you come back."

"We was quiet, wasn't we?" Luke asked.

"You were very quiet." She met Jake's gaze past Luke's head and exchanged a small smile with him. They both knew the boys had been as quiet as could be expected.

The ranchers waited until the door closed behind Mrs. Sperling then resumed their conversation.

Hannah ducked into the kitchen, but even there, she could hear every word.

"Should've known Murphy'd do something like this when he refused to join us in settling a price and said he intended to ship his cattle further up the line rather than pen them with us. Murphy stands to turn a nice profit if he's the only supplier." Hannah knew Martin said the words. He struck her as an angry man. "We ought to get together an outfit and take care of this the old-fashioned way."

"Knowing and proving aren't the same," Jake said, his voice hard.

"I suggest we drive our cattle to where Murphy has his and provide him some stiff competition," Riggs said.

"It's a waste of time and money," Jake said. "What we need to do is prove to Mr. Arnold the animals are healthy."

"And how do you propose to do that?" Martin demanded.

Hannah knew the continual thudding sound was Martin pounding his fist into his palm. "I could send a couple of my hands to persuade him."

"I'll send him a telegram informing him he's been mis-informed," Jake said.

The other two laughed.

"Mr. Arnold always struck me as a reasonable man," Jake added.

There were some grunts, and then Riggs said. "Let's do it, then."

Boots clattered across her polished wooden floor. There came the thud of the door swinging shut, and then blessed quiet.

Hannah returned to the lobby and looked around. If she stripped the smoke-stained wallpaper from behind the desk, she could replace it after the Sperlings paid her. She tried to concentrate on how their leaving would give her cash to buy new wallpaper. But she kept thinking how quiet it would be without Mrs. Sperling to visit with, the little boys to amuse her, and Jake to—what? Annoy her? Make her wish for something she once had? She tossed the idea away. Nothing about Jake and his life even vaguely resembled what she'd had.

Overcome with homesickness, she hurried to her room. She opened the top drawer of the chiffonier and dug under her stockings until she found a small case.

four

Hannah sat on the edge of the bed and opened the black case. Her vision blurred as she ran her fingertip over the pocket watch her father had left her. It had two tiny diamonds mounted on it. Everything else of value had been sold to pay bills after his death. Even the house had to go to the bank. Her father had gone heavily into debt providing Hannah and her mother with nice things. Things they didn't need. Or at least she didn't. She wasn't so sure of her mother. It seemed she couldn't deal with the harsh realities of fending for herself even though Hannah had promised she could manage for the both of them. No doubt it explained why her mother accepted Otto's offer of marriage as soon as her mourning period ended. But for Hannah, security at the cost of her independence constituted too high a price. She'd never told her mother how demanding Otto had been. *Thank You, God, for giving me a way out.*

She blinked away the tears. She had only to pick up the watch to see her father, hear his voice as he told her he was proud of her, and smell again his unique scent of oil and produce from working in his store. She could still hear him praise her independent spirit.

She closed the case and shoved it back out of sight. She would fix up this hotel and return it to the profitable business it had been for her grandparents. Her father would be proud of her.

She marched back to the kitchen, armed herself with hot water and a scraper, and headed for the lobby to tackle removing the wallpaper.

It proved to be a messy, sticky job. She had half the wall left to do when Mrs. Sperling returned.

As Hannah started to climb off the ladder, the older lady stopped her. "We've already eaten, and I think we're ready for an early night."

Hannah knew the boys were tired when they accompanied their grandmother up the stairs without protest. The cookies would have to wait until tomorrow.

She returned to her task, attacking the sooty paper with a vengeance. She'd show Jake she could do this. She had to prove herself equal to her father's expectations.

"Seems every time I turn my back, you climb a ladder."

Hannah, startled at the sound of Jake's voice, steadied herself, relaxed her tense grip on the scraper, and turned to see him leaning against the desk, grinning. "It's part of the job."

"At least you aren't perched on the top."

Hannah glanced at the remaining corner and decided not to finish it while she had an audience. She climbed down, wiped her hands on a rag, and used her arm to brush her hair out of her face. She wouldn't look at her reflection in the windows to see how mussed she had become. But she felt a bit of paper in her hair and flicked it away.

He grinned and picked out a few pieces. "How long have you been at this?"

"Since you left." A big clock hung next to the stairs, and she looked at it and gasped. It was long past suppertime and almost dark out.

"It doesn't all have to be done tonight, does it?"

She brought her gaze back to him, surprised at how weary he sounded. "Seeing I'm my own boss, I can do it whenever I want." She said it airily, but until she got the place ready to open, she had no income.

He grimaced. "Being the boss means you never get to relax. Mother and the boys?"

"They went upstairs hours ago. Haven't heard a sound since."

"Then I don't have to worry about feeding them." He stretched.

"Did you get your business taken care of?"

"We sent a telegram asking the buyers to come see for themselves. Don't expect we'll hear back until morning."

"What happens if they won't come?"

He rolled his head back and forth and rubbed at the back of his neck. "I suppose we go find them ourselves. Riggs and Martin are all for dragging Mr. Arnold out by the scruff of his neck."

"And what do you think?"

"It took me hours to round up some feed for the animals. And it's only enough for one day. I just want it over with so I can get home and take care of things." His stomach rumbled loudly. "Sorry about that."

"Haven't you eaten?"

"Had to check on Mother and the boys first. I'll go find something now."

Hannah checked the time. "I doubt anything will still be open."

"I'll have to wait for breakfast, then."

"I haven't eaten, either. There's enough for two—" She hesitated. Would he be willing to share her meager fare again?

"You're sure?"

"I wouldn't ask if I wasn't." She headed for the kitchen then turned back, realizing Jake hadn't moved. "Come on. You're welcome to join me."

He tossed his hat on the desk, brushed his hair back with his palms, and followed, hesitating in the doorway. "Remember, I'm not real good in a kitchen," he murmured.

She laughed. "Not to worry. I can manage on my own."

He nodded and sat at the far end of the table.

She stirred the fire to life and put the kettle on the hottest part of the stove and tried to decide what she could make for him. In the end, she fried eggs and potatoes and served biscuits left from the day before.

He reached for her hands as he bowed to pray.

She wanted to pull back, not wanting to get even remotely close to him. He objected to her independence as strongly as Otto had. But it seemed childish to refuse to hold his hands as he prayed, so she turned her palms into his, noticing the roughness of them, the way they seemed to overpower her and yet still feel so gentle.

When he said, "Amen," he didn't immediately release her.

But Hannah couldn't keep her head down forever and slowly brought her gaze up to his. She saw warmth in his brown eyes and wondered what he felt.

Then he smiled. "Thank you for this."

She nodded, ducked her head, and concentrated on her food.

❧

Jake savored the potatoes, crispy and salted to perfection, and the eggs with runny yolks just the way he liked.

Maybe if he itemized the merits of the food, he'd stop

thinking about how her hands had felt—small, yet firm and strong. Not unlike the woman herself, he guessed.

Hannah puzzled him. Why did she insist she could fix this place by herself? The smell of smoke persisted in every corner. He swung off his chair and closed the pocket doors to the dining room.

She questioned him with her eyes.

"Thought it might keep out some of the smoke smell."

"I guess I'm used to it."

He wanted to protest she shouldn't have to get used to such a thing but knew she'd take objection to his interference. Still, why should she? What was she trying to prove? He stuffed half a biscuit in his mouth to keep from asking.

She'd said something about her father. As if he would approve. He couldn't imagine any man willingly allowing his daughter to take on such a task. "What happened to your father?" At her startled expression, he added, "I know he died. I'm wondering how."

"Pneumonia."

"Oh." His mind flooded with questions, but a man could hardly blurt out things like, "How long did it take? Did he suffer?"

"It was mercifully quick," she said, answering his unspoken questions.

"That's a blessing."

"I suppose you're right, though it didn't seem like it at the time. I thought my world had ended. In some ways it did. My father had gone into debt to build a big house. I guess he thought that's what Mother wanted."

"Did she?"

She shrugged. "I shouldn't speak poorly of her, but it does

seem she prefers comfort to independence. It's the only reason I can think of for her marriage to Otto."

Jake tried to digest that. His father had made him promise he would always see that his sister and mother were kept comfortable. He assumed that's what a man did for a woman. But Hannah made it sound less than second best.

She chuckled. "I'm afraid Otto bit off more than he could chew when he got me in the bargain. I'd sooner be less comfortable and more independent."

"Independence carries a price—responsibility."

In the dim light her eyes looked dark and bottomless. He could feel her thoughts reach out to him and dig deep into his heart as if trying to fathom his meaning. For a moment, he thought she would acknowledge the truth in his words, but she only chuckled. "Comfort can carry a price, too. Especially if it means being controlled by another's desires. I'll take the alternative."

Disappointed by her stubbornness, Jake swiped his plate clean and leaned back. All sorts of arguments crowded his mind, proofs she was wrong, but at the set of her mouth he guessed she didn't care much about proof.

She went to the cupboard and pulled some cookies from a tin, placed them on a plate, and put them on the table. "The boys were so tired tonight they didn't even stop for cookies. I'll have to be sure they get some before they go out tomorrow."

He jerked forward. "I suppose Mother wore herself out, too?"

Hannah smiled. Her eyes twinkled. "She seemed glad enough to go to her room."

He glanced at the ceiling, wondering if he should check on her.

"I'm sure she's sound asleep by now," Hannah said.

He pulled his attention back to her. Why did she grin so widely? Just looking at her made him smile in response. He liked the way her eyes crinkled at the corners. He wanted to pick out the flecks of wallpaper peppering her hair but guessed she might object to such a bold move.

She blinked before his stare. "Tell me about your father." Her voice sounded husky. "Your mother said he had an accident."

"Yeah. Gored by a bull."

Her eyes widened. She sucked in her breath in a quick little motion then didn't seem to be able to let it out. She scrubbed her lips together two, three times, and then air escaped her lungs like a hot wind off the dry plains. "How awful."

"It wasn't pretty."

"I'm sorry. And you were still young."

"I don't remember being young." He had grown up really fast after his father's accident. "My father died inch by inch in agony, but he never stopped being in charge. And in the months he lived, he taught me everything I'd need to know to take over." He'd learned long ago to speak of it without feeing anything, to think of his father's death with emotional detachment. A man had to move on from such things, concentrate on his responsibilities. There wasn't room for weakness. His father had taught him well.

"Does it seem strange to you that your father's death gave you more independence and responsibility than you wanted and my father's death deprived me of mine?"

"It's not more'n I can handle."

"Of course not." Her eyes carried unspoken disagreement.

He wanted to prove her wrong. It had never been more than he could handle. He would never falter in his responsibilities.

"And you've bitten off more than you can chew." He circled his head, indicating the hotel.

She fiddled with her napkin a moment then fixed him with a solid stare. "As you said, it's not more than I can handle."

He didn't want to agree. In fact, the more he got to know Hannah, the more he wanted to protest. But somewhere between the fried potatoes and the last crumb of cookie, things between them had shifted. And he didn't want to spoil this new feeling—like the moment a horse stops bucking and realizes it can either fight or cooperate. Bad example. Yet somehow it fit. He and Hannah had somehow, somewhere in the discussion, silently, mutually, he hoped, agreed they could be friends. Not wanting to spoil that flush of understanding or whatever he decided to call it, he refrained from saying anything about the hotel.

He pushed his plate aside. "That was good. Thank you." He rubbed his hands over his thighs.

She narrowed her eyes. "Aren't you going to toss me some more coins?" She breathed hard.

"Why would I do that?"

"You did last night."

He tried to remember. Riggs and Martin had stormed in, ready to do business. He'd gone with them to meet the train, expecting the buyers. Had he unthinkingly dropped some money on the table as he normally would when eating out?

He had. "I wasn't thinking."

"I suggest you do so in the future."

"I apologize."

She considered him for a moment then nodded.

He thought she meant to say something more, but a bell clattered somewhere in the distance.

Hannah bolted from her chair. "Someone's in the lobby. Can't anyone read the closed sign?" She pushed the doors open and headed across the dining room.

Jake quickly stood. "Watch the hole in the floor." Someone was going to get hurt. He followed her, skirting the hole.

The lobby, lit only by the light from the kitchen, lay in shadows. A cowboy clung to the desk, swaying as he leered at Hannah crossing the room. "I's here for room," he slurred.

Hannah took her place behind the desk. "I'm sorry. We're closed."

The cowboy swung his head around to stare at Jake, the movement almost tipping him over. He grabbed the desk, pulled himself upright, and turned back to Hannah. "Aw, lady. Bet ya can find me a room somewhere." He leaned over the desk, leering again.

Hannah stepped back. "No sir, I can't. But I'm sure the Regal will have a room for you."

"Wizened-up old guy runs the place. Not like here." He grabbed for Hannah, but she ducked out of his reach.

Jake had seen enough. He crossed the room in three strides. "Cowboy, you're done here." He kept his voice low, but the young man jerked up, not missing the sound of an order. Jake squeezed the man's elbow and accompanied him to the door. He fought the temptation to shove him into the street.

Even so, the cowboy stumbled and almost fell.

Jake watched, knowing his wish to see the boy flat on his face in muck was not very Christian. He slammed the door and turned the lock. He faced Hannah.

She hugged her arms around herself, her eyes wide and dark.

"Did he scare you?" he asked.

She shook her head. "Not at all."

His insides burned at her denial. "He was drunk. He might have hurt you."

"I don't think so. I'm not completely helpless."

"You're alone here. How did you think you'd stop him?"

"Just because I'm not a man doesn't mean I can't take care of myself."

This helpless feeling when he thought about her situation—wanting to protect her, knowing she resented his suggestion that she needed it—had been simmering since he'd seen her on the ladder and caught her as she fell. It reached the boiling point as the drunk threatened her. It now seared through his insides and spilled over. "He's bigger, stronger than you."

She reached under the desk and pulled out a bat, brandishing it like a sword. "I'm not entirely unprepared."

He pulled up straight and stared at her. His hot, humorless surprise made him laugh. "A bat? Do you think he was going to throw a ball?"

"I'd pretend his head was a ball."

With two steps, he quickly closed the distance between them.

She must have seen the anger in his eyes or guessed at it. She started to back away.

He shot his arm out and snatched the bat from her hand. "Now how would you stop him?"

Even in the poor light he could see he'd made her angry. "I wouldn't try. I wouldn't have to. Because"—she stalked to the desk and leaned over, pushing her face so close he eased back six inches before he could stop himself—"I wouldn't be here. If I was open—and I'm not—Mort would be at the night desk."

"Your fine-sounding argument didn't keep that cowboy out."

"I normally keep the door locked after dark." She leaned forward another inch. "It's only unlocked tonight because I had to wait for you to come in."

He pushed his face closer. "Don't be so stubborn. This is not a safe place. The work is too much, the risks too great, the—" He forgot his third reason as he breathed in the scent of wallpaper paste from her hair and a whisper of something so sweet he thought of fields of wildflowers so full of nectar a thousand bees danced in joy. His gaze dropped to her mouth. His thoughts skittered so wildly he couldn't begin to capture them.

Hannah pulled back. "You are gravely mistaken, Jake Sperling, if you think I can't do this. I can and I will."

He reined in his thoughts. He had never before in his life felt the desire to shake a woman until her teeth rattled. He stuffed his hands in his pockets. "When you find you can't, I'll help you pick up the pieces."

She snorted. "I suggest you don't hold your breath waiting."

He smacked the bat onto the desk and stalked up the stairs.

&

Hannah waited until she heard his door shut. Only then did she sag against the desk. The drunk had frightened her. But it wouldn't happen again. In the future she'd be sure the door was locked or Mort was at his job as night clerk.

She went to her room and sank to her bed. Shivers ran up and down her spine. She opened her Bible and read for a few minutes. Finally, admitting the words weren't making any sense, she closed her eyes and prayed. *Thank You, God, for keeping me safe.* She just wished it hadn't been at Jake's hands. Why was he so determined to see her fail? Didn't he have enough to worry about with his own family and his ranch to run?

She went to the chiffonier again and pulled out the case containing her father's pocket watch. She pressed it to her chest, forcing her thoughts away from the drunk, and with a little more effort, away from Jake. She focused on what her father would have said. "My independent little girl, you know your mind. I like that. Don't let anyone tell you you can't do it."

He'd encouraged her independence. He admired the quality in her. It had become her defining characteristic.

She returned the case to its place and prepared for bed. Under the covers, she whispered another prayer. "God, please help me not fail."

❧

Hannah woke the next morning, her determination solidly in place. She quickly went to work on the hotel.

Mrs. Sperling and the boys came down as Hannah mopped the lobby floor.

"Do you have our cookies?" Luke yelled.

Hannah was beginning to wonder if one of their parents had difficulty hearing. That would explain why they felt the need to talk at the top of their voices. "I promised them cookies yesterday for being so good," she told Mrs. Sperling.

"Why don't we go find breakfast then come back for tea and cookies?" their grandmother asked.

The boys screamed their delight at the idea.

"Do you mind?" Mrs. Sperling asked Hannah.

"That would be fine." She glanced up the stairs.

"Jake left to see if the buyers had come on the early train. He's worried about the cows." The older woman shook her head. "I can't understand why the buyers haven't come. I'm sure Seth could have persuaded them."

Hannah wanted to protest. Jake had surely done his best. But it wasn't any of her business, and she turned back to her work as Mrs. Sperling left with the boys.

The lobby cleaned, she headed upstairs to tidy the rooms the Sperling family used. She finished that task and returned to the main floor.

The door opened and three men in suits entered.

"I'm closed," she called.

"We're not wanting rooms," one said, "but we are here on business. Are you Miss Williams?"

"I am." She hurried over to the desk, feeling the need to look official. "How can I help you?"

"Allow me to introduce myself." The first man stepped forward. "Mayor Stokes." He bowed slightly, his bowler hat pressed to his chest. "These two gentlemen are Mr. Wass and Mr. Bertch, members of the town council. Mr. Bertch is also the safety inspector."

They nodded, shifted from foot to foot, and avoided her gaze.

Hannah told herself she had nothing to be concerned about, but still every nerve in her body went into quivering attention. "To what do I owe this honor?" Maybe it was a welcoming committee.

Mayor Stokes, apparently the official spokesman, pulled a paper from his pocket. "It's about the fire. Or should I say the water bill from the fire."

She blinked. "What do you mean?"

The mayor harrumphed. "As you know, or being new in town perhaps you don't, the town is dependent on well water for its supply, and we have instituted a policy that if people exceed reasonable use, they should pay for it."

"Really. Who determines what is 'reasonable use' and when it is exceeded?"

"Why the town council, of course. It's part of our job."

The other two men nodded vigorous agreement.

The mayor continued. "We almost pumped the well dry dowsing your fire. Here's your bill." He shoved the piece of paper toward her.

At first she didn't take it, but he shook it demandingly. She opened it and read the amount and gasped. "This is outrageous."

Mayor Stokes looked as if she'd personally called him a blackguard. She hadn't, but she began to think she'd be correct if she did. The other men found something very interesting to study on the wall behind her.

She pressed her lips together to keep from sputtering. "Could you be so good as to tell me when this water rationing policy came into effect?"

The mayor ignored her question. The other two continued to study the wall. Their silence was answer enough.

"Is that all?" she demanded.

"There's one more matter. I told you Mr. Bertch is the safety inspector. He's here to inspect the hotel."

Hannah's cheeks grew hot. Her stomach tensed. "My hotel is not open for business yet. When it is, it will pass any sort of inspection."

Mayor Stokes blinked several times. "I understood you have guests here right now."

The Sperlings. She could hardly deny it, though they'd practically forced her to allow them to stay. "Temporarily," she muttered.

"Then Mr. Bertch is obligated to conduct his inspection."

The three of them marched toward the dining room. Mr. Bertch pulled out a pad of paper and pencil and began to make notes. Hannah knew he had no need. The damage was plain, as they must know. Everyone in town knew.

He circled the room, Mayor Stokes and Mr. Wass treading on his heels. He barely glanced into the kitchen, returned to the lobby, and pretended to inspect it. Only his gaze went up the stairs.

"Miss Williams, this place is not safe for habitation."

five

"It will be," she protested. "I need time to fix it." Time, money, and supplies.

The three men put their heads together and muttered, and then Mayor Stokes faced her. "We'll give you three weeks to pay the water use fine and complete the repairs. If they aren't complete then we'll be forced to impose further fines." He cleared his throat. "We're being more than generous. We could condemn the place today and board up the door."

Mr. Bertch dropped a paper on the desk; then the three marched toward the door.

Hannah read the notice they left:

THIS IS TO INFORM MISS HANNAH WILLIAMS
THAT THE SUNSHINE HOTEL MUST PASS
A SAFETY INSPECTION IN THREE WEEKS' TIME
OR BE FINED A HUNDRED DOLLARS.

Her cry of outrage brought Mort from the backyard. "Problems, miss?"

She waved at the paper on the desk as she hurried to her room to think this through in private.

She sank to the edge of her bed. It seemed obvious the mayor and his associates had targeted her, but why? Was it the money, or did they want her out of town? Maybe like Jake, they thought it wasn't a job for a woman.

She looked at the drawer holding the little black case. Her father would expect her to handle this. But how? She considered her choices. Quit? Not an option. Ask for help? Briefly she let her mind swerve toward Jake. Would he help her if she asked, or side with the town fathers? Probably the latter. That left her with one alternative. She had three weeks. In that time, she had to get the hotel ready for occupancy and earn enough to pay the water bill.

She headed back to the lobby and stood looking around. With a little bit of wallpaper, it would be presentable. Why couldn't she take in guests with the same arrangement she had with the Sperlings? Reduced rates because the dining room wasn't available. If she had the dining room door closed off, surely Mr. Bertch couldn't condemn it as unsafe? It would be inconvenient for her to have to go outside to get to the kitchen, but if it meant having paying guests, she would do it.

She marched up the stairs to study the eight unoccupied rooms, all with considerable smoke damage. She knew much of it could be scrubbed away with soap and water—and lots of elbow grease. Well, she'd better get at it.

She persuaded Mort to take down the drapes from the first three rooms and hang them outside to air. She'd try sponging them later in the day. She carried the ladder upstairs then, armed with hot water, soap, and lots of rags, headed for the first room.

"Miss Hannah. Miss Hannah." The siren sound of two little boys rang out.

She dropped her cloth in the water and went down to serve the promised tea and cookies.

ख

The next day was more of the same. Mrs. Sperling took the

boys out for breakfast then returned for tea and cookies. Other than that, Hannah spent every spare moment scrubbing and cleaning. She caught glimpses of Jake as he hurried in and out. According to Mrs. Sperling, he hadn't been able to persuade any of the buyers to come and spent his day trying to find feed for the cows.

She had three rooms scrubbed and their bedding stripped down to the mattresses. She didn't have to bury her face in the ticking to realize they'd need a good airing. She wondered if Mort would do it, but he'd been at the desk until late last night waiting for Jake to return. She'd promised him she wouldn't disturb him. That left her to do the task on her own. She tugged a mattress off the bed. It was unwieldy but not heavy. Surely she could get it down the stairs.

She pushed, pulled, and dragged it to the hallway, got it to the top of the stairs, and then paused to catch her breath and consider her next step. She could drag the mattress, but if it got away on her she'd be pushed down the stairs. Nope. Better to push it down than have it push her. She got behind and shoved. It clung to the carpeting. She pushed harder and managed to get it to the top step. Somehow she'd figured it would dip down the stairs. Instead it merely stuck out. She pushed some more. It still stuck out. She kept pushing but couldn't believe how the mattress continued to defiantly stick out over the steps.

Hannah gave one more hearty shove, and the mattress flipped flat, dropping its full length to the steps. She bent to grab the sides, hoping to control its descent, but it took off. She fell to the padding as the mattress gained speed. She clung to the edges. *Bump, bump, bump.* She felt every step in her chest, then her stomach, knees, and toes. As she realized the trip down the steps was going to be slow but bumpy, her initial alarm gave way to amusement.

The mattress reached the polished wooden floor and picked up speed. Hannah giggled. This was fun. She laughed harder. If anyone saw her now, they'd think she'd gone crazy. Maybe she had, but she hadn't laughed like this in a long time. And it felt good.

At that moment the door opened and Jake strode in. She barely had time to holler, "Look out," before the mattress struck his ankles and ground to a halt.

He teetered a minute like a tree cut down at its roots, waved his arms madly, and then toppled, landing beside her.

Laughing so hard tears filled her eyes, Hannah rolled away.

"What are you doing?" He was obviously not amused.

She tried to stop laughing, but the harder she tried the harder she laughed.

He grunted and sat up. "Don't tell me Luke and Sammy are up to mischief."

She shook her head. "Just me," she managed to gasp as she sat up and faced him. Seeing the look of disbelief on his face, she again laughed.

He looked from her to the top of the stairs then shook his head. "Why are you riding mattresses down the stairs?"

She stifled her laughter. "It was unintentional, believe me. But fun." She got to her feet and brushed her hands over her hair. She must look like a wild hooligan. But she didn't care. For the past three days, she'd done nothing but work and worry about this hotel. In fact, in the month since she'd arrived, it had been nothing but work. Like Jake once said, being the boss meant never having time off.

"Care to tell me what you were trying to do?" Jake asked.

"I wanted to get this mattress downstairs so I could take it outside and air it." She chuckled.

He scowled, obviously still not amused.

She tried again. "If I'd known it was so much fun, I'd have done it sooner."

Nothing but a frown. "Where's Mort? Why haven't you asked him to help you? Are you so set on proving how independent you can be that you're willing to risk life and limb?"

"Oh, come on, Jake. I didn't get so much as a scratch. See." She held out her arms and turned them over for his inspection. Ignoring his grunt, she chuckled. "I think God knew I needed to remember life is supposed to be fun. I was getting all caught up in work."

"How many mattresses are you planning to bring downstairs?"

"Eventually all of them, but right now I'm concentrating on three rooms."

He headed for the stairs. "Show me which ones."

"No need. I can do it myself."

"You might not be so fortunate next time." He continued up the stairs with Hannah at his heels.

"Which rooms?" he demanded at the top of the steps.

She indicated the ones. "I need to get the rooms ready to let out as soon as possible. Sooner, even."

He hoisted a mattress to his shoulders and edged his way out the door. "Seems you have a lot bigger problem than the mattresses."

"What do you mean?"

"The hole in the middle of the dining room floor."

"I plan to close the room temporarily. Surely there will be those who would take the rooms at a reduced rate." She counted heavily on it.

"I suppose so." He carried the mattress through the dining room and out the back door and propped it against the shed wall then headed back for the third mattress. She followed him.

When he paused at the top of the stairs with the mattress balanced on his shoulders, she asked, "Sure you don't want to try riding it down?"

He shot her a look. "Not in this lifetime."

She followed him again. "It was awfully fun."

"I'll take your word for it." He propped the mattress beside the first, retrieved the one from the lobby floor, and then stood back and dusted his hands. "You didn't say where Mort is."

"Doing his own thing, I suppose. I can't expect him to work day and night."

"Either get him to take these back upstairs when you're ready or wait for me."

She'd never planned to carry them up on her own, but his bossiness irked her, and she couldn't resist letting him know she didn't need him to run her life or her business. "And if you or Mort isn't here? Do you expect me to drink tea and twiddle my thumbs until one of you returns? You're sadly mistaken if you think I'm going to pretend to be a helpless female who flutters her fan and waits for a man to pick up her hankie."

They'd reached the dining room, and he jolted to a halt and studied her long and hard.

She tore her gaze away. She'd been rude, and she tried mentally to justify her behavior. "What you don't understand is I haven't time to waste. The town council paid me a visit. I have no choice but to get this place up and running before—" She bit off the rest of her explanation. She hadn't planned to tell anyone about the visit. She found it humiliating to confess just how close she felt to desperation.

"Mayor Stokes and his cronies were here? What did they want?"

"Nothing." She headed for the lobby, leaving him to stare after her or follow—whatever his inclination.

He followed, grabbed her arm, and turned her to face him. "What did they want?"

She set her mouth. It was none of his business.

"Has it anything to do with us being here?"

She stared at him, reluctant to reveal anything.

"I could persuade Mother to move."

"Don't do that." She needed the money for paint, paper, and a hundred other things.

"Then tell me what's wrong."

She pulled away and sat at the little table where she'd served them. "I've been fined."

"You broke the law?"

She laughed. At least he sounded suitably disbelieving. "Apparently there is a penalty for the overuse of water, which this fire caused."

"I didn't think you were even here at the time."

"I wasn't, but as owner of the hotel I have the dubious pleasure of qualifying for the fine."

He snorted. "How wonderful. So you plan to reopen soon? What about that hole?" He nodded toward the dining room.

She explained her plans. "Only one thing bothers me. The safety inspector could choose to say it isn't good enough." She ducked away from his study of her. Hannah knew before he spoke what his solution would be. Still it annoyed her when he gave it.

"Hannah, why are you doing this to yourself? You could sell the place or at least hire a manager or—"

"You mean admit I can't manage on my own? I'd never do that."

"What are you trying to prove? Everyone has limitations. It's not weak to admit them."

"I think it bothers you to think a woman can get along without a man."

"Why would you want to?" His voice was low. His eyes bored into hers.

She realized they weren't talking about the hotel anymore but something more basic. Something involving only the two of them.

Did she want to be without a man? A man who loved her and cherished her, even maybe took care of her? Somehow her father had been able to do both yet still encourage her independence.

She had only to let her thoughts drift a breath away from the present to remember his returning home in the evening, smelling of the store. She could see him backlit against the open door then coming into focus as the door closed behind him. She felt again the anticipation of watching him hang his hat and shrug out of his jacket. Only then did he turn to her and Mother. He kissed his wife and hugged Hannah. She could hear his words in her memories: *And what worlds did you conquer today, Hannah?* He loved to hear of her adventures.

"I'd like to marry someday. Have someone to share my life." She missed having someone be as pleased to see her, as proud of her accomplishments as her father had been. Her missing took on solid shape that sank, heavy and cold, to the bottom of her stomach. She would welcome the same acceptance from a man she could love and spend her life with. Could she ever hope to find the same thing with a man her own age?

Certainly not with Jake. He ruled his world. And she did not want to be ruled.

Jake glanced at the clock and jumped to his feet. "I'm going to miss the train. Tell Mother I've gone to find the buyers and convince them to come here. I'll be back day after tomorrow." He dashed up the stairs, returned with a carpetbag, and with a hurried good-bye headed out the door.

&

Two days later, Hannah was scrubbing yet another room, wondering why she had the feeling she waited for something. Her mind pictured Jake. It wasn't as if she missed him. She'd known him only a few days. Hardly long enough to have given her cause to hurry to the window when she heard the late afternoon train yesterday. Even knowing he didn't plan to return until today, she had waited long enough to be sure he hadn't changed his mind before she'd returned to her work.

She was still cleaning upstairs when she heard Mrs. Sperling and the boys and went down to join them. She glanced past them to see if Jake accompanied them and scolded herself yet again.

"We went shopping," Luke announced in his wild hog-calling voice. "Gamma bought us new shirts. Can I show her mine, Gamma?"

Mrs. Sperling handed over a package wrapped in brown paper. The two boys tore at the paper and pulled out two store-bought blue shirts. Each held one up in front of him.

Hannah admired them. "Now why don't you sit down, and I'll get cookies and tea?"

Mrs. Sperling already sat at the table, her chin resting on her upturned hands. "That would be nice, dear."

The boys pulled out chairs. Sammy managed to upset his

backward, and the two of them worked together to right it.

Chuckling, Hannah left them to sort themselves out as she headed for the kitchen to make tea. She put out a good number of cookies and carried a tray back to the lobby. She poured a little weak tea into cups of milk, passed them to the boys, and offered them cookies. They each took two. Then Hannah turned her attention to pouring tea for Mrs. Sperling.

"Thank you, my dear."

Hannah glanced at the older woman. Her cheeks were pale, her eyes glassy. "Are you feeling well?" she asked.

Mrs. Sperling closed her eyes. "I'm afraid I have a headache." She grimaced at Hannah. "A real one this time."

Sammy yelled something about the horses he'd seen on the street, and Mrs. Sperling flinched.

"Boys, talk like gentlemen," Hannah warned.

Mrs. Sperling shivered.

Hannah touched her hand. "It looks like you should go to bed."

Mrs. Sperling opened one eye and looked at the boys. "I can't take my eyes off them."

Hannah knew the older woman could barely keep her head up. "Why don't I take them for the afternoon?"

"I couldn't—" Mrs. Sperling began.

"It will be fun." She'd learned her lesson with the mattresses. Work could not be the shape of her life. She had to make room for fun as well. Besides, she had four rooms ready except for washing the bedding, and she intended to do that on Monday. "Why don't I take them out?" They'd been confined long enough. So had she. She wanted to see what lay beyond the streets and houses of town.

"I'd be so grateful," Mrs. Sperling whispered.

"Then it's settled." She touched Luke's chin to get his attention. "How would you two like to go exploring today?"

"Yeah!" they both yelled.

"Finish your cookies and tea." She shooed Mrs. Sperling upstairs, found Mort, and informed him of her plans, laughing when he looked as if she'd announced she intended to drive nails through her fingers. "We'll have fun."

"Yes, miss," he murmured, obviously not convinced.

❧

Jake didn't wait for the train to stop before he jumped to the platform. It had been a long day and a half, but he'd finally convinced Mr. Arnold to visit and assess for himself whether the rumors of sick cattle were founded. The man had promised to show up Monday morning. Two more days for Jake to cool his heels and chomp at the bit.

He waited for the conductor to push open the boxcar door where his horse rode. As soon as the animal stepped out, Jake threw on the saddle, took care of his bags, and arranged to have a message delivered to Riggs and Martin. Only then could he head for the hotel. He'd check on his mother and the boys before he checked on the animals.

Inside the lobby, he knew from the quiet the boys were not on the premises. He cocked his head toward the stairs, listening for sounds of Hannah hard at work. But there was only silence.

Mort shuffled in from the kitchen. "Your mother is upstairs resting. Had a headache. Not much wonder with all the racket."

Jake nodded. "Audrey hasn't come for the boys, then?"

"No sir."

He tensed. That left the boys unsupervised. "Then where are they?"

"Miss took them."

"She say where?"

"Out of town, she said."

"Thanks." He decided to leave his mother in peace and headed outside. Out of town... That included a lot of territory. Where would she take them? She could manage the boys. She'd proved that time and again, but she didn't know the country. What were they doing? But instead of disaster, he pictured her chasing the boys, catching them, and tickling them, or perhaps playing beside a stream, throwing rocks into the water.

How long had it been since he'd done something for the sheer enjoyment of it? Too long to remember. Too long to matter. Seemed his whole life he'd been taking care of business. Trying to live up to his daddy's expectations.

"It's a big job," his father had warned him from his deathbed. "A man-sized job, but I've taught you well, boy. You can do it. Just don't be distracted by foolishness. You won't have time for it. Not even the things a boy your age would consider normal."

Jake rode to the herd. Zeke had managed to keep them fed and watered. The animals looked fine.

So how foolish would it be to ride out and find Hannah and the boys and maybe enjoy a few quiet hours? He chuckled at thinking there'd be anything quiet about an afternoon spent with his two nephews.

He rode as far as the feed store. Lars stood on the step talking to a customer. He glanced up at Jake's approach. "You looking for Miss Williams and the two young 'uns?" Before Jake answered, the man pointed down the road. "She asked how far to the river. I told her to follow her nose."

"Thanks." Jake let the horse amble along the dusty trail.

Occasionally he glimpsed three sets of footprints.

As he drew close to the river, he heard the boys' voices and turned aside. He tied the horse to a tree and edged forward to watch Hannah and the boys play. They stood on the edge of the river, throwing rocks. Sammy saw one he wanted just below the surface of the water.

"Take off your shoes and socks," Hannah said.

Jake slipped closer.

Both boys sat down, pulled off their shoes and socks, and rolled up their pants. They were soon knee deep, bent over, and up to their elbows in water as they tried to wrench rocks from the river.

Sammy tripped, fell to his bottom, and struggled against the current.

"Hang on. I'll get you." Hannah took a step forward then hesitated. She pulled off her own shoes and stockings, wadded her skirts up, and headed toward the boy.

Jake guessed she meant to help Sammy. He could have told her the boy was fine, but he preferred to enjoy the entertainment.

As she reached for the boy, she lost hold of her skirts and they swirled around her, sinking as they took on water. She paused, looking back as if wondering if she should retreat.

Jake found himself silently urging her on. Now was no time to play it safe.

Suddenly she laughed, grabbed water, and tossed it above her head. Then she splashed the boys. "No point in trying to keep dry now."

Jake leaned against a tree, smiling as the boys squealed then began to flail at the water. For a few minutes he could hardly see them through the spray.

He caught glimpses of Hannah as she retreated. Water beading on her skin caught the sun making her appear to be sprinkled with diamonds. Her hair fell from the coil she usually wore and hung in dark, thick ropes down her back. Her face glowed with laughter.

Suddenly Jake felt old and alone.

Hannah, tossing water into the air and laughing, didn't seem to notice the boys closing in on her.

Jake jumped forward. He knew what happened when Sammy tackled people around the knees. They fell like big old trees in a high wind. He reached the water's edge the same time Sammy reached his target. "Hannah," he yelled.

But she tipped backward, seemed to lie on top of the water for a heartbeat, then folded and disappeared under the surface.

His brain kicked into a gallop. She might be caught on the bottom, hampered by her clothing or unable to pull herself free from Sammy's clutches. He strode into the water, pushing through the resistance. He reached the place where she'd gone down just as she emerged blowing out water and scrubbing her hair out of her face.

"You trying to drown me, Sammy?" She laughed.

Jake grabbed her shoulders and dragged her to her feet. "You scared me."

She gasped and clutched his forearms to steady herself. "Where did you come from?"

He jerked his head in the direction of his horse but kept his gaze on Hannah, enjoying the way her eyes lit with recognition then shifted to confusion.

"How long have you been here?"

"Long enough to see you playing in the water."

She grinned. "I was being very responsible. Making sure the boys were safe."

"Such a wearisome task." He caught a strand of her wet hair and dragged it off her cold cheek and then felt her sharply indrawn breath. He paused, considered dropping his hand to his side, reconsidered, caught another strand of hair, and lifted it off her face.

Her eyes widened, reflecting the bouncing light off the running water and gentling it into something warm. She drew in a breath that seemed not quite steady to him. "No reason a person can't enjoy her responsibilities."

"First I heard about it." He again watched her emotions fill her eyes and shift through a range from amusement to surprise and then to mischief. He noticed the latter a second too late as two soaking bodies tackled him. "Uncle Jake, play with us."

He staggered under their assault and grabbed at Hannah to catch his balance. He knew immediately he'd made a mistake and pulled his hands away and let himself fall.

Unbalanced by his attempt to steady himself, Hannah splashed down beside him, sputtering as she took in a mouthful of water. She dragged herself upward until she sat swaying in the water.

Jake struggled against Sammy and Luke, who seemed intent on drowning him. "Boys," he yelled, "get off me."

Instead of obeying, Sammy sat on his chest and Luke on his legs.

"See my rock," Sammy yelled, shoving a small boulder in Jake's face.

"Nice rock," he grunted as he fought to a sitting position. "What're you going to do with it?"

"Keep it."

Why would he want to keep a rock? More specifically. . . "Where will you keep it?"

"On my pillow."

Hannah chuckled. "Nothing cute and cuddly about his pets."

"Audrey will probably let him, too."

Luke splashed his hands in the water. "I'm all wet," he announced.

Jake stated the obvious. "We all are." Suddenly it struck him what a picture they made sitting fully clothed in the middle of the river having an ordinary conversation. Something deep inside his gut started to rumble and build. It tickled at his insides and bubbled upward until he roared with laughter.

The boys grinned and started to giggle, and Hannah joined in with her musical laugh.

Jake laughed so hard his eyes teared. No one would ever know, though, as water trickled down his face from his wet hair. He laughed until he felt weak and his stomach hurt. He couldn't remember when he'd laughed so hard. It made him feel like his insides had been scrubbed.

Still chuckling, he pushed to his feet, pulled Hannah up, and then grabbed a boy in each hand. "Come on. Let's get out of the water." On the shore he worked off his boots and drained out the water, scrubbed his hands over his hair, and let his clothes drip. He watched as Hannah twisted and squeezed her long dark hair.

Seeing his gaze on her, she gave an uncertain little laugh. "I'm a mess."

He wanted to say he'd never seen anyone more beautiful, but his mouth had developed a temporary case of lockjaw. He could only manage a little grin and a shake of his head.

She must have read something in his expression that gave

her a clue to his thoughts, because she lowered her head, hiding her face behind the curtain of hair.

Jake thought it was a good thing she didn't realize the gesture made him even more tongue-tied.

She stole a glance at him through the fringe of her moisture-beaded eyelashes.

He'd had girlfriends. He knew of the natural attraction between a man and a woman. Seen it in others. But what he felt with Hannah went far beyond that to something more personal, more special, more demanding, yet comforting. He felt as if their hearts had jumped from their chests and danced together in the bright sunshine.

He jerked his gaze away and pressed the heel of his hand to his forehead. The cold must be affecting him, making him fanciful. Downright foolish, in fact. "Good thing the sun is warm," he murmured as he turned to watch the boys racing up and down the bank of the river, collecting more rocks, leaves, and twigs.

"Uncle Jake," Luke called, "help me get this rock."

Glad of the diversion, he hurried to help Luke pull a rock from the grass. He could see nothing special about the rock. It was just black, mottled with white specks.

Luke, however, peered at it proudly. He grunted and tried to pick it up. "Uncle Jake, can you carry it for me, please?"

So Jake bore it back to the steadily growing mound.

Hannah met Jake's eyes. He thought he saw a questioning warmth in her eyes, as if she, too, had been aware of the moment of connection between them. If she had, did she know what it meant? He didn't.

Hannah turned to Sammy as he lugged another rock to the pile. She gave the boy the same gentle look he imagined he'd seen in her eyes when she looked at him. He'd been foolish in hoping—

He brought his thoughts to a halt. He hadn't been hoping for anything. His life was already full to overflowing. Last thing he needed was someone else to take care of. He turned away and stared unseeingly at the river. Like Hannah needed taking care of. She'd made it plain she took care of herself.

Hannah laughed softly, making him forget who needed or wanted caring for. "What are you building?" she asked the boys.

"A mountain," Luke announced.

Jake resisted an urge to slap his forehead. Luke wasn't the only one building mountains. Jake had been doing so in his mind. Turning an innocent bit of play into something bigger and more important than it could ever be.

six

Hannah shook the sand from her wet skirts, wishing she could as easily shake the confusion from her brain.

Why had Jake joined them? It didn't seem as if he'd come to check on her, which she would have understood. Instead, he seemed intent on having a good time.

She'd never heard such heartfelt laughter as Jake produced sitting in the middle of the river with two small boys crawling on him. It was a long laugh in the right direction and made her feel happy inside. Just remembering it brought a smile.

But thinking how he'd looked at her caused her smile to slide into something softer, less amused, more—she shook her skirts harder. More what? What did she think she saw in Jake's eyes? What did she want to see? She didn't know, but she felt achy inside. Like tears had built up somewhere behind her heart. She sensed if they escaped they would flood her insides. Her skin couldn't contain all she longed for.

She missed her dad. She missed her mom. She missed something she'd never had. She didn't even know what to call it.

She swung her wet hair over her shoulder. Time to stop being silly. No need to let a little jocularity affect her normal good sense. She longed for nothing more. She had her independence and a hotel full of opportunities.

She turned back to the little boys piling up rocks. "It will take a lot of work to build a mountain. You're going to need some help."

She searched along the shore, found a rock, marched over to the "mountain" the boys were building, and added to it.

As she and Luke gathered rocks, Jake stood looking at the river. She paused to study him. Did he have troubling thoughts similar to hers? She snorted softly. He was probably thinking about his cows.

Sammy bounced up to Jake. "Uncle Jake, give me a piggyback ride."

Hannah waited to see Jake's response. Part of her saw him as the big, unapproachable, in-charge boss. She still had a hard time accepting his warmth toward his family. Warmth and caring and—something more. She searched for the right word. *Responsibility*. That was it. He wore his responsibility like a shirt covering every other emotion. Maybe it explained his attitude toward her. Her independence simply did not fit into his frame of mind.

He scooped up Sammy and hung the boy around his neck then raced up and down the shore, bouncing the boy until he screamed with laughter.

Hannah smiled. She liked this relaxed Jake much better than the one who seemed to think he had to be in charge of everyone in his sphere. But which one was the real Jake?

They had each dried to a wrinkled mat when Jake glanced at the sky. "It's time we got back."

"Aww," Sammy and Luke yelled together. They stood in front of their stone "mountain," now as high as Sammy's waist.

"Uncle Jake, what we going to do with our rocks?" Luke demanded.

"I wanna take them home," Sammy screamed.

"You can't haul rocks home," Jake protested.

Luke stuck his bottom lip out. "Why not?"

Hannah chuckled at Jake's quandary.

He shot her a helpless look. "Luke, there are lots of rocks at home."

"We want these ones, don't we, Sammy?"

The younger boy nodded vigorously.

Hannah giggled as the two small boys and one large man glowered at each other. The whole lot of them had stubborn streaks a mile wide and bright as polished gold. If someone didn't intervene, they could wrangle at this for a long time. She swallowed back her amusement and put on a serious face. "Boys, why don't you each pick out the rock you like the best and take it home. Leave the rest here. I'm sure you can come back and visit sometime."

Three pairs of eyes shifted toward her then toward the stack of rocks. Jake opened his mouth.

Fearing he might order the boys to obey her suggestion and likely trigger their stubbornness rather than their cooperation, Hannah went to the rocks. "Which one is your favorite, Sammy?"

The boy squatted down and studied the rocks with such concentration, Hannah had difficulty not smiling. "I like 'em all," he said. But he selected five and set them on the ground at his feet. "These are my favorites. Can't I take 'em all?"

"No," Jake muttered.

Hannah ignored him. "Can you carry them all?"

Sammy tried, but even with Hannah's help at balancing them in his cradled arms, he couldn't manage five and looked about ready to cry. "They're so nice."

"Maybe you can take three," she suggested.

So with much deliberation, he chose three. " 'Bye, rocks," he said sadly to those remaining.

Luke crossed his arms and refused to follow his brother's example.

Hannah rose and faced Jake. "I guess Luke doesn't want to take any. That's fine. His choice. Shall we be on our way?"

Jake grabbed the reins of his patient horse, muttering, "Why are you encouraging them? Who needs to carry home rocks?"

She chuckled. "I think they'll give them up without an argument after a few steps. On the other hand, if they want to pack them all the way, what difference does it make? Might keep them out of trouble."

Jake suddenly laughed. "If it does, I'll be surprised."

Luke waited until he realized they were indeed headed home then grabbed two good-sized rocks and followed.

For a moment they walked in relative silence. "Relative" meaning she and Jake didn't speak and the boys yelled endlessly about new treasures discovered along the trail. As she'd predicted, they soon ditched their rocks in order to pick up something more exciting.

The boys' clothes were spotted with mud and wrinkled. Her own blue cotton dress, one she normally thought rather attractive, was now bedraggled and dull with sand and dust. She glanced at Jake—his trousers stained, his blue shirt streaked from its dunking in the river. She chuckled. "We're a rumpled-looking crew."

He glanced down at himself, groaned, and then swept his gaze over her. "You've faired better than I."

Uncomfortable with his grinning assessment, she shifted her attention past him to the dusty haze along the trail. "How did your business go? Did you get everything settled?"

"I hope so. Mr. Arnold said he'd come out Monday morning and assess whether the cattle are healthy as we claim."

"Then you achieved what you intended. You must be pleased."

They strode on for several paces, the horse plodding along behind them, before Jake answered. "I'm happy enough that he's agreed to come, but this delay never should have happened. I should have foreseen the possibility of Murphy doing something and been a step ahead of him."

Hannah heard the frustration in his voice but wondered why he blamed himself. "How can you be responsible for something another man has done?"

"It's my job to be sure things go well."

"But Jake, you can only be responsible for what *you* do."

He made a noise she took to be disagreement before he spoke. "That's easy for you to say. You're set on proving just that. Responsible for no one but you, to no one but you, but I have others to think about, plan for, and make sure they're taken care of."

"You make my choices sound selfish. I don't see them that way. By becoming independent, I'm giving my mother and stepfather the chance to start a new life together without my being caught in the middle. And I'm honoring my father's memory by living up to his expectation of me."

She again heard that noise that seemed to come from deep inside him. Not a grunt. And yet definitely negative in tone. "I would think your father would want what's best for you."

Her vision narrowed as she regarded him through squinted eyes. "Of course he would."

"Then he would probably suggest you ask for help fixing the hotel."

She shook her head. "He'd expect me to figure out how to do it myself."

They stopped walking and faced each other.

A few days ago, Hannah would have erupted at Jake's interference, his continued insistence she couldn't manage on her own, but she began to suspect his problem stemmed from his own overgrown sense of responsibility. He seemed to think it was his job to take care of everyone. "Jake, it isn't like I'm entirely on my own."

He widened his eyes. "I thought—"

"I am God's child. He will never leave me nor forsake me. Hasn't He also promised to provide all our needs?"

"Well of course, but doesn't the scripture also say, 'If any provide not for his own, and specially for those of his own house, he hath denied the faith, and is worse than an infidel'? Doesn't that make our responsibility plain? It seems you have only yourself to think about, so I suppose that verse has no significance for you. For me, it's the guiding direction for my life."

Hannah knew the scripture he mentioned but had never heard it applied the way he did. "It seems to me you feel like you are personally responsible for things that are beyond your control. Aren't there times you have to let God do it? Trust Him?"

"I do trust Him. I trust Him to help me take care of the task set before me."

Hannah and Jake resumed walking side by side. She turned her attention to the two little boys hunkered down, examining something in the dusty tracks, before saying, "That's exactly how I feel. God has given me the desire for independence and now the means. I trust Him to help me take advantage of the opportunity He's provided."

Jake made that same sound of disagreement but didn't voice his feelings, for which Hannah was grateful. She had no desire to argue and ruin the enjoyment of the afternoon, though she suspected it would come to an end as soon as they were back in town. Jake would revert to the man in charge of everything. His ranch. His cows. His men. His family. Did he also feel responsible for friends and acquaintances?

That would explain why he felt he had to tell her she couldn't manage on her own. But she could. And she would. She'd prove it to Jake. Not that it would be her motivation. She wanted to live up to her father's expectations of her, prove worthy of his approval and thus honor his memory.

"Wagon coming," Jake said. "I'd better corral the boys." He lengthened his stride and caught up to Sammy and Luke, who were watching a caterpillar crawl through the dry grass at the side of the road.

Hannah hurried to them and held Sammy's hand as Jake held the reins on one side and Luke on the other.

The rattle and rumble of the wagon grew louder as the wagon approached and passed. The driver waved and called a greeting, and then Hannah turned aside to shield her face from the cloud of dust.

"Where's he going?" Luke demanded.

"He's taking supplies to settlements west of here beyond the railway," Jake answered.

"Can we go see?" Luke asked.

Hannah chuckled as the man and boys stared after the wagon as if accompanying it in their thoughts.

"We have to get back to town before Grandma starts to worry." Yet Jake didn't move.

Luke stood beside him. "Who lives out there?"

"Mostly miners, but I suppose farmers, ranchers, and townspeople, too." The wagon turned a corner and disappeared from sight, but still Jake and Luke stared down the road.

Sammy pulled away from Hannah's grasp and went in search of the caterpillar. She shifted so she could keep an eye on the younger boy yet watch the other two. It seemed they had both been mentally drawn away by the passing wagon.

"I heard there are big caves in the hills to the west," Jake said.

"I want to see them," Luke replied.

"It's too far." Jake led the horse and boy back to the road and waited for Hannah to fall in beside him. The caterpillar had disappeared, and the boys ran ahead in search of new discoveries. "I always wanted to see the caves," Jake said then sighed. "Don't suppose I ever will."

"Why not? Don't you deserve a holiday?"

"I'm the boss."

"Exactly. If you want to go see caves, you put someone else in charge and go."

He shook his head. "You've been boss of your business how long? A month? You'll soon find that being the boss doesn't mean you just sit around and give orders."

She laughed at his assessment. "I could shout orders all day long, but there's no one but Mort to hear me, and he does what suits him. But you have people who can help. I've seen some of your men. They appear very capable. So why don't you go see the caves?"

Luke had joined them. "Uncle Jake, can I see the caves, too?"

Jake laughed. "If I go, I promise to take you."

"Sammy, Sammy, we're going to see the caves," he screamed, racing toward his brother.

Jake caught Luke around the waist. "Hold up there, young man. I said *if* I go. Truth is, I don't plan to go, so you'll have to wait until someone else can take you."

Luke scowled at his uncle as he squirmed out of his grasp and stomped down the road, leaving little clouds of dust in his wake.

They soon arrived in town and turned the boys over to their grandmother, who had recovered from her headache.

Halfway across the dining room, Jake caught up to Hannah. "Let me take you out for dinner."

She ground to a halt. "Dinner?" They'd just spent the afternoon together and argued about the differences in how they viewed the world. They would always argue, because he would never accept her independence and she would accept nothing less. "Why?"

"You need a reason to consider an invitation from me?" He sounded shocked.

"I suppose you're accustomed to people seeing your invitations as orders?"

"Now that you mention it…" He chuckled. "Of course not. But I thought you might enjoy a nice dinner at the Regal."

She'd stolen glimpses through the window as she passed but knew she couldn't afford such luxuries. "I'm rather a mess."

"I am, too, but we could clean up."

Still she hesitated. She couldn't honorably accept an invitation just to get a free meal. Inside her, in a spot deep beneath her heart, something else urged her to say yes. Even though she knew they could never be more than friends, and not even good friends, not with his attitude toward her independence, something about this man appealed to her—his strength of character.

The very thing making it impossible to relax around him proved to be what she admired the most and the very reason she should refuse his invitation. But although she informed her brain of this fact, her mouth said, "I'd love to. Give me an hour to clean up."

&

Jake held the chair as Hannah took her place in the Regal's dining room. She'd cleaned up really nice. She'd brushed her hair until it shone enough to make him think of a mink he'd once seen. He fought an urge to touch it to see if it were as smooth and soft as the animal's fur.

She wore a snowy white blouse with a narrow pin at the neck with some sort of clear stone that caught the light and shafted it into a rainbow of colors. Could it be a diamond? He hardly thought so. A woman who owned diamonds wouldn't be scrubbing smoke-damaged walls.

She nodded her thanks as he pushed the chair in for her. He took his place across from the table, hoping he'd cleaned up as nicely as she. He'd chosen a white shirt with a black string tie and his best black trousers. He'd even cleaned and polished his boots until they gleamed.

She leaned forward, smiling. "This is as nice as I imagined. All the white linen and sparkling white china." She took her time looking around the room. "Maybe someday my dining room will be as nice."

The waitress handed them menus, sparing him from speaking the words springing to his mind—that he doubted she would ever get her dining room usable, let alone fancied up like this one.

"Roast turkey. Sounds good." He hoped they provided large servings. He was starving.

"Sounds good to me, too," Hannah said.

The waitress filled the crystal water goblets and took their orders. Jake wished for something a little sturdier for his big hands but gingerly took the glass and sipped his water, unable to think of anything to say.

Hannah leaned forward. "See that old couple over there? He's so sweet. Look at the way he tries to please her." She watched them.

Jake kept his gaze on Hannah, wondering about her observation. "The old gentleman is taking care of his wife," he said. "Seems contrary to your stand on independence."

She slowly brought her gaze back to him. "Not at all. A person can be thoughtful and gentle and caring without robbing another of the right to make her own decisions. My father taught me that. There wasn't a more thoughtful man." She turned back to watching the older couple. "In fact, if he'd lived, I can imagine him and Mother like that."

He waited for their meals to be placed in front of them and inhaled the rich aroma of turkey and dressing, mashed potatoes and gravy, and a mound of peas and carrots. "A dead father, idealized, makes for stiff competition for any man." He knew he could never measure up to the standard her father set. Not that he wanted to. A woman like Hannah would be constantly challenging him. Life was complicated enough without asking for more trouble.

She concentrated on her meal for a moment. "I would never want anyone who didn't make me feel special like my father did."

Jake thought he saw sadness, regret even, in her eyes. "How did he do that?"

"He encouraged my independence. Told me I could do anything I set my mind to. At the same time, he—" She paused as if searching for the right word. "It's just that I knew I was special in his eyes." She turned back toward the older couple. "Just like that."

Seemed she had expectations no man could ever meet. It irked him. "You're the only child?"

"I am."

He recalled what she'd said about her mother. Seems the mother liked being taken care of. Hannah was less like her mother and more like— Jake narrowed his eyes. More like a son. "Did your father regret not having a son?"

She smiled. "If he did, he never said so."

To Jake, it seemed her father had tried to turn Hannah into the son he never had, despite the impossibility of disguising that she was a very pretty young woman. Those thoughts were best kept to himself.

She edged forward. "I thank God every day for allowing me to come west."

He studied her. She was a woman made to be cared for. She shouldn't be trying to clean up a burnt-out hotel that would challenge Zeke and half a dozen of his men. A man's job was to take care of such a woman, but determination blazed from her eyes. He stifled the argument building in his chest and fought the idea he wanted to take care of Hannah. He knew she wouldn't let him. Wouldn't even entertain the notion.

He filled his mouth with dressing, letting the sage flavor sift through his senses.

"Don't you find it awfully quiet?" Hannah whispered. "I seem to have gotten used to Sammy and Luke's volume of conversation."

He gave an expansive sigh. "It's bliss. Their noise is always a shock to my hearing. I don't know how Audrey and Harvey put up with it." He paused. "Or why. Seems they could have just as much fun without bringing down the roof."

"Your poor mother is about at the end of her patience with them."

"I know. Thank you for helping her as much as you have. It's a good thing we go home Monday. Even if Audrey isn't back, at least Sarie is there to help. She's our cook and also a good friend."

Hannah put her hands beside her plate and took a deep breath before she looked at him again. "So you will be leaving soon?"

"Monday. As soon as the cattle are sold." He wondered if she would miss him—them. He thought of his nephews' noise. If she missed them, it would no doubt be mixed with gratitude for the peace and quiet. "I hope Mother doesn't overtax herself in the meantime."

"It will be awfully quiet with you all gone." Her gaze held his. Went deep into his heart as if she sought something in him. Then her expression grew friendly but impersonal. "I'll miss the company."

His, too? Suddenly his brain flooded with wishes for things that could never be. Sharing more discoveries with this woman. Sharing laughter. Sharing enjoyment. Sharing each other's loads.

He turned to watch a young couple take their places at a table near the door.

Hannah did not want anyone to share her load. Nor did he need any more responsibilities.

The waitress took away their plates, replacing them with generous portions of apple crisp drowned in thick, farm-fresh cream.

He inhaled the scent of apples and cinnamon and prepared

to enjoy the tasty dish when he heard Hannah suck in air like someone had hit her. He turned his attention back to her.

Eyes wide and glistening with tears, she choked out a whisper. "The last time we dined at a restaurant as a family, my father ordered this dessert."

He placed his hand over hers and squeezed. "I'm sorry. You must miss him a lot."

She nodded. "I thought I was over this. After all, it's been four years. But every once in a while something hits me and it's like it happened yesterday."

He wondered if she knew she'd turned her hand over into his palm. If they weren't in public, he'd have pulled her into his arms and held her. Despite her protestations, she needed holding and protecting.

"I guess I've been thinking of him more than usual because I feel like I'm finally living up to his expectations for me."

He couldn't fight her dead father. And she didn't seem to be able to let the man go.

She shuddered once, pulled her hand away, and then took a mouthful of the dessert and smiled. "It's good."

He had no reason to feel he'd been shoved out into the cold because she no longer reached for him. He watched the young couple, whispering together, flashing smiles as they spoke, and clasping hands across the table. He guessed they were fresh off the farm from some settlement to the west and thrilled by this new experience. He smiled at the way the girl's eyes widened at each new thing—the fine goblet, the steaming plate of food, and the silver teapot the waitress served from.

Hannah noticed his attention. She, too, smiled. "I bet they're newly wed," she murmured, "with eyes for no one else."

"They're noticing all the new things around them, though."

Jake pulled his gaze back to Hannah at the same time she looked toward him. His heart gave a peculiar leap he couldn't explain as if trying to escape his chest, as if stretching toward Hannah. A fleeting thought raced through his numb mind. *Will she ever consider giving up her freedom to become someone's wife?*

The waitress appeared at his side to ask if she could remove the dishes and inquire if they wanted anything more. He answered her without looking away from Hannah. "Are we done?" he asked but barely waited for her to answer before he shoved his chair back.

She nodded.

He hurried around to pull back her chair.

She paused to straighten her skirts.

They turned as the young man made a hoarse sound.

"I don't have enough money," he whispered to the girl across from him. "I must have left the rest in the hotel."

Hannah looked with shock-filled eyes toward Jake.

He took her elbow, steered her toward the exit, and left her waiting at the door as he went to pay the bill. He gave some extra money and spoke quietly to the waitress. "This is to pay for the young couple over there. Tell them God's best on their new life together."

As he and Hannah made their way out to the dusk, he took Hannah's hand and pulled it through his arm, telling himself he meant only to steady her in the darkening street. He felt rather pleased with himself when she didn't protest. "Do you want to go with me to check on the herd?" he asked.

"I'd love to."

They tramped along the sidewalk until they reached the end then crossed the street and made their way to the pens.

Shorty had built a fire, filling the dusk with dancing shadows. Jake paused at the rail fence and breathed in the familiar, comforting smell of the animals. He expected Hannah to withdraw her hand.

Instead, she pulled him around to face her. "I saw what you did for that young couple. You were very kind." Exerting gentle pressure on his forearm, she leaned forward, raised her face, and kissed him on the cheek.

He couldn't believe it happened. Then a stampede of emotions raced through him. Emptiness finding its fullness, heart finding heart with a matching rhythm. He wanted nothing more than to hold this woman and keep her safe and protected. He slipped his arms around her shoulders and stared into her eyes, half hidden in the dim light. "Hannah," he whispered. Slowly, hesitantly, giving her plenty of opportunity to refuse, Jake lowered his head and kissed her.

The warmth of her lips went straight to his heart, where a gate exploded open, revealing yearning for a love of his own and loneliness he'd denied over and over. He slammed shut the gate. Dropped his arms to his side. Letting himself get too fond of Hannah presented major complications. Stubborn, independent, and determined to run a derelict hotel. He backed away. Time to pull his head together, or was it his heart that needed corralling?

"I better see if Mother is coping with the boys." He turned his steps toward the street and waited for Hannah to join him.

He'd been so busy with his own thoughts he hadn't given her any study. Now he did. She avoided looking at him as she pulled her arms around herself as if she felt suddenly cold. He half raised an arm to pull her close and protect her from the elements, dropping it again without touching her. No reason to think she might have had the same jolting reaction to his kiss. She likely had other things on her mind.

They murmured mindless comments about the weather and the town as they returned to the hotel. They barely made it through the door before he bolted for the stairs, claiming an urgency to make sure things were under control in the rooms his mother shared with his two nephews.

seven

Hannah's first waking thought had been to leap from bed and hurry out to the lobby. Jake checked the herd every morning. Maybe he'd ask her to join him. She wanted to spend every minute of the day with him. Tomorrow he'd be gone—along with his mother and nephews. She would be alone again except for Mort, who really didn't count as company.

She wanted to selfishly enjoy this, their last day. She had no illusions that once he got back to the ranch and his responsibilities he would give her another thought. They both knew they didn't fit into each other's worlds.

Her second thought kept her in bed staring at the white sheet blocking the early morning sun. It was Sunday—no reason to hurry out of bed. She wouldn't be doing any work. And after her foolish reaction to Jake's kiss last night, she'd be wise to avoid him.

She pressed her fingertips to her lips. Of course, she couldn't still feel his kiss. But she hadn't forgotten how she'd felt. She shifted her hand to a spot over her heart. She massaged gently, trying to ease the tightness, knowing the tension wasn't in her chest, nor in her muscles, but in her emotions. She felt safe in his arms. Felt a sudden urge to let go of all her burdens.

She blew out her lips. What burdens? The hotel was her ticket to independence and as such, a welcome challenge, not a burden.

She slipped from the bedcovers and prepared for church. If

she took extra pains to look nice, it was only her self-respect as a businesswoman, not because she hoped Jake would notice.

She heard the boys yelling as they came down the stairs, heard Mrs. Sperling call to them, and then heard Jake's deeper voice ordering them to be quiet.

Hannah's heart broke into a breathless gallop, all her mental admonitions instantly forgotten. She had only to hear his voice for the tightness in her chest to return.

She remained in the kitchen, waiting for them to leave. She'd follow later, slip into the church unnoticed, and escape the same way. She couldn't face Jake, try and make ordinary conversation, when she had to keep fighting herself.

She went to the mirror over the cupboard and stared at herself. "Hannah Williams, you know what you really want. It's to open this hotel, become independent. Nothing less will ever satisfy you. No use in pretending you'd be happy being something you can't be. You can never be what Jake wants—a woman to take care of."

"What do *I* want from a man?" she asked her reflection. She recalled the words she'd spoken to Jake. *A man who would treat her as her father had. Cherish her while allowing her independence.* She pointed her finger at her reflection. "And that, Hannah Williams, is not Jake."

"Hannah." The sound of Jake calling from the dining room caused her to spin away from the mirror. "Are you coming to church?"

Her heart soared. He wanted her to accompany them. She grabbed her Bible and hurried out to join him. "I'm ready."

Not until they were striding down the sidewalk toward the little white clapboard church at the north end of town did she realize she'd ignored her own advice to keep away from Jake.

They went inside the bright interior and slowly made their way down the aisle, pausing to speak to friends and neighbors—the Sperlings doing most of the greeting. Hannah knew only a handful of people yet.

Mrs. Sperling slipped into a pew with the two boys. Hannah started to follow, but Jake guided her into the bench behind them. She squeezed in beside Mrs. Johnson, and Jake lowered himself to her side. She shifted to give him more room, acutely aware of the pressure of his shoulder against hers. Though if he were three pews away, she would have been equally aware of him. She knew gratitude when the pastor stood and announced the first hymn.

She loved church. Loved singing with the others. Loved hearing God's Word. But as Jake's deep voice joined hers, she knew enjoyment she'd never felt before. They shared the same hymnal. She didn't look at him. Didn't need to in order to sense he shared the same pleasure in singing songs of the faith.

The preacher opened his Bible. "Our scripture for today is First Samuel, chapter seven, verse twelve. 'Then Samuel took a stone, and set it between Mizpeh and Shen, and called the name of it Ebenezer, saying, Hitherto hath the Lord helped us.'" He spoke of God's faithfulness to His people in the past and the assurance of His continued help and guidance in both the present and the future.

Peace filled Hannah's heart. She was here because God had given her the gift of a hotel, a way to leave the confines of her home with a new stepfather and a chance to become all that God intended.

She rose after the benediction, renewed by the message, and smiled at Jake. "I expect you'll have much to do today."

"Not really. Mother and the boys have been invited to visit friends for the afternoon."

"The cows?"

"All taken care of."

They exited the church and stood in the warm sun. "A quiet day for you then?"

"Would you care to have lunch with me?"

"But nothing is open."

He glanced after his mother. "I suppose we could go with Mother and the boys."

She laughed. "You sound excited about that."

"I'm not. Too much noise."

She hesitated. A whole Sunday afternoon alone held no appeal, but another day with Jake. . . Her emotions were already in enough turmoil. But telling herself she felt sorry for him, she said, "I could put together a few things and we could have a little picnic."

"Excellent."

He accompanied her back to the hotel and stood outside as she gathered up a few simple things for a lunch. "If I'd known about this yesterday I'd have baked a cake," she said softly so he wouldn't hear. No cake. Three-day-old cookies would have to do. And cheese sandwiches. An afternoon in the sun would surely make up for any lack in the food.

She wondered if they would go toward the river again, but he headed the other direction, past the church to a grove of trees. The sound of muted voices informed her it was a popular spot. They wouldn't be alone. *Good*, she told herself, stifling her sense of disappointment.

He spread the blanket she'd brought, and she passed him a sandwich.

"Did you enjoy the service?" she asked.

"I did, though I miss our little church out at the ranch."

"You have a church out there?"

He chuckled. "We're actually quite civilized."

"I didn't mean it like that. I just never thought. . . Well, I guess I thought it was isolated and. . .I don't know. I've never been to a ranch, so I'm not sure what it would be like."

"We'll have to remedy that, won't we?"

At the soft tone of his voice, she darted a look at him, intending only to steal a glance. But their eyes collided, and she couldn't pull away from his bottomless brown gaze. Did he mean his words as an invitation? Would she welcome it if he did? Wasn't it best to forget this unlikely attraction between them? "I've always lived in town," she murmured as if expecting him to see how far apart their worlds were.

"I guess you'd never be able to live on a ranch."

His doubts as to her adaptability forced her to say, "I could do just about anything I made up my mind to do."

He searched her gaze as if trying to determine exactly what she meant. She wondered herself. She couldn't define what she thought or how she felt, other than it gave her a sensation like swinging too high, her breath catching on the upward arc, holding there after she'd begun the downward flight, catching up with her body just in time for it to repeat. She sucked in air, heavy with the scent of leaves getting ready for autumn, and pulled her thoughts together. "Tell me about your church."

He chuckled again and turned away to pick a cookie from the tin. "It isn't *my* church even though it's on my land. Father built it as soon as he finished the house. Said they needed a place to worship. He wanted his outfit to have the option without traipsing off to town."

"What does it look like?"

"It's small. Constructed of logs like the house. Father made sure there was lots of light. The windows are clear so you look out on trees on one side and rolling hills on the other. I'd sooner worship outside, but the church isn't half bad, either."

"It sounds beautiful. What about a preacher?"

"Pastor Rawson, the preacher you heard earlier this morning, comes out in the afternoon."

Hannah fiddled with a leaf that had fallen by her knee. "Tell me about how you became a Christian."

Jake took two more cookies and leaned back against the nearest tree. "I can't remember not knowing God loved me. One Sunday when I was about seven, a warm spring day I recall, I simply decided I wanted to join God's family, and I went to the church after everyone had left from the service and knelt at the front."

Hannah's throat tightened with emotion as she pictured a young Jake making his choice all alone. Seems from an early age he stood alone and strong. "It sounds very special."

"It was. Still feels special."

Again they looked deep into each other's eyes. Hannah felt a connection beyond ordinary interest. This man had deep spiritual roots to accompany his strength of character. A person could safely lean on him. She sighed. His mother and sister were fortunate to have him.

"How about you?" he asked.

For a moment she thought he asked if she wanted to lean on him, too. But he didn't know she'd been thinking it. "Me?"

"How and when did you become part of God's family?"

Her breath gusted out. "I, too, always knew God loved me. But I had more of a struggle. I didn't want to give up my independence to belong to Him."

Jake laughed hard and earned himself a frown. He stopped laughing and looked suitably serious, though his eyes danced and the corners of his mouth twitched. "I can see that might be a problem. How did you resolve it?"

She grinned. "I didn't. God did. I'd been taught to read my Bible every day. I read some verses that made me willing to give up my ways because I knew I could trust God to do what was best for me. They're in Romans chapter eight. 'And we know that all things work together for good to them that love God, to them who are the called according to His purpose.' And 'He that spared not His own Son, but delivered Him up for us all, how shall He not with Him also freely give us all things?'" She smiled from the depths of her heart. "He loved me enough to give His Son to die for me. I guess He wouldn't do anything that wasn't for my good."

Jake took her hand. "Amen."

Hannah knew that more than their hands connected. They'd shared from their faith experience, and a bond of deeper understanding had been forged.

A zephyr blew through the treetops, rustling the leaves, sending a shower of them to the ground. Hannah shook her head to get them out of her hair.

"Hold still," Jake said, leaning close. "One's stuck in your hair." He gently eased the leaf from its perch. "It's like a golden crown." His voice seemed thick.

She felt his fingers working loose the leaf. Felt a thousand sensations race from her scalp to her heart.

He released the leaf and tossed it to the ground.

She didn't look up. She couldn't free herself from the longing in her heart—a longing to be held and cherished.

"Some gold dust left behind," he whispered, flicking his fingers through her hair.

She closed her eyes and thought of letting herself love this man.

She sucked her breath in and sat up straighter. "Thanks." She didn't belong in Jake's world where he dominated, controlled, took care of—gently touched her hair. No. No. He didn't belong in her world, where she expected to be cherished but also given freedom to make her own choices. She turned to put the lid on the cookie tin. She knew one subject that would pull them both back to reality. "I've got four rooms ready to open in the hotel, plus the suite will be available when you and your mother and the boys leave tomorrow."

He dropped his hand, picked up a twig, and broke it into inch-long pieces and tossed them aside. "What about the dining room?"

"I'll get Mort to board it off tomorrow."

"Seems you'll have to fix it sooner or later."

"It will have to be later. I think I'll be ready to put an open sign out by Tuesday."

"That's great." He stood, waited for her to put the picnic things in the bag, and folded up the blanket.

She felt him pulling away from her. She'd ruined the afternoon. But she had no choice. They both needed to stick to reality. Yet she regretted it ever so slightly. About as much as she would regret denying herself Christmas.

They returned to the hotel, and he handed her the blanket. "Thanks for the picnic. I have to check on the cows." He strode away without a backward glance.

She went inside, stared at the hole in the dining room floor, and wondered what it would be like to live on a ranch. She shook her head. She had no time for dreams of romance, especially with a man like Jake. She had a hotel to fix and run. It was her dream come true.

ঽ

The last animal jostled into the boxcar, and Shorty pushed the door shut.

Jake shook hands with Mr. Arnold. "Nice doing business with you."

"Sorry about the misunderstanding," the man said.

Martin and Riggs stood at Jake's side. He heard Martin's grunt, but thankfully, the man kept his opinion silent and avoided alienating the man they hoped to do business with again.

They shook hands all around.

Jake told the cowboys to head back to the ranch, and he swung to the back of his horse. At the livery barn he told Con to bring the wagon. Once the supplies were loaded, he could be on his way home. He couldn't wait.

He paused outside the hotel door. He didn't look forward to saying good-bye to Hannah, though in effect they'd said it yesterday. He didn't want to leave her here on her own, yet she'd made it clear as the sky above that she wanted nothing more from him. There wasn't room in her life or heart for a cowboy like him. Saying good-bye today would simply be a matter of paying the bill, shaking hands, and parting ways.

He pushed the door open and strode in. Mother sat in the lobby, the bags packed and ready. Looking after the boys for a few days had meant this stay in town turned out to be less of a holiday than he'd planned for her. She should have told Audrey to take her children with her, but Mother never could say no to Audrey. And to keep from upsetting his mother, he usually gave in, too.

Mother glanced past him. "What did you do with the boys?"

He checked the room. Saw no boys. "What do you mean?"

Mother grew pale. "I told them they could wait for you outside. Made them promise not to go past the corner."

"I didn't see them. The little rascals must have hidden." He threw the door open and bellowed, "Luke, Sammy, where are you?"

Mrs. Johnson, sweeping the steps in front of the store, paused to look at him.

"Have you seen the boys?" he asked.

"Not since earlier this morning when your mother took them out for breakfast."

"Thanks." He called them again. Nothing. He returned inside. "They're not out there. Maybe they're with Hannah." He strode into the dining room, noticing she'd removed the damaged tables and chairs and pulled the rest to one corner. The hole gaped like a cave, and he got down on his knees to look inside. No boys. "Hannah," he called again as she wasn't in the room. Jake continued his search.

He found her outside, stacking the chairs and tables for Mort to burn. "Are the boys with you?"

She jerked around to face him. "Haven't seen them since they came back from breakfast with your mother. Aren't they with her?"

"No." He wanted to brush the soot from her cheek and finger the strand of hair curling around her ear.

She looked toward the back door. "Are they playing a game?"

"I expect so." He hurried to the lobby, Hannah hard on his heels.

"I'll check the kitchen," she said.

"I'll look outside."

Mother sat up. "I'll—"

Jake held up his hand. "Wait here in case they come back. Then don't let them out of your sight."

He and Hannah returned in a few minutes. At the shake of her head and the worry in her eyes, he knew she'd had no more success in finding the pair than he.

The three adults turned toward the stairs. Jake took them in three bounds and searched their suite thoroughly. He didn't find his nephews.

Hannah stepped into the hall as he considered where to look next. "They aren't in any of the rooms up here," she said.

"They have to be hiding outside. I have to widen my search."

Hannah reached the bottom of the steps as quickly as he. "I'll help you look," she said. Her hard tone made it plain she wouldn't take no for an answer.

He chuckled. "Don't think you'll stop me from giving them a good bawling out."

She grinned then jerked her gaze away as together they headed for the door.

They searched and called. An hour later, Jake's frustration had given way to anger that dissolved into worry. "Where could they be?" He envisioned them sneaking into some little outbuilding and the door shutting on them, trapping them inside. But they'd gone up and down the alleys calling and listening and searched every conceivable hiding place.

"Maybe they're staying one step ahead of us," Hannah suggested. "If we split up we might catch them."

"We'll outsmart them. You go that way, I'll go this, and we'll meet back at the hotel."

But an hour later, back at the hotel there were no little boys. And Hannah hadn't returned.

He strode from one corner of the hotel to the other. He went outside again, jumped into the middle of the street, and glanced up and down the length. He started toward the railway tracks, stopped, and retraced his steps. He had no idea where to look for Hannah or the boys. But he couldn't simply wait.

He headed back down the street. He stopped in every store opening and asked if anyone had seen Hannah or the boys. He even stepped into the lawyer's office and asked. He knew Hannah wouldn't play games. But where was she? Why hadn't she come back? Was she hurt? Or worse? His stomach clenched into a twisted knot. How could the three of them disappear? How could he have let this happen?

❧

Hannah searched every store, checked behind each counter. She knew how mischievous the boys could be. No doubt they thought this was a fine game. But it was no longer fun. She thought of all the things that might have happened to them. Maybe a runaway horse had struck them. But the whole community would have heard about it. Maybe they had fallen somewhere and been hurt. But unless they were both unconscious they could yell loudly enough to bring help from the far corners of this little town. It was almost impossible for them to get lost.

So where were they?

She stood in front of the general store and tried to figure out what they would have done. A dray rumbled to the store and stopped. Another wagon headed west. She'd heard one earlier in the day. A big shipment must have come in on the last train. The driver jumped down and went inside.

Wagons. West. Caves. She remembered how anxious Luke had been to see the caves. Could the boys have—

She raced into the store where the wagon driver purchased a

handful of candy. "Mister, can I get a ride with you?" She tried not to think how big the man was.

"Ride to where, ma'am?"

"You're headed west, aren't you?" At his nod, she asked, "Are there caves out there?"

"Heard there was. Never seen 'em, though. I'm headed to Fall River. Little settlement."

"That will do. Do you mind a passenger?"

He studied her hard, openly. But thankfully, he didn't leer. "You running away?"

"No sir. But I think two little boys might have stolen a ride on the last wagon. I have to find them."

"Sure thing. You come along with me. We'll find Frank and ask him if he seen the lads." He held out a hand as big as a mitt. "I'm Jud."

She gave her name, let him take her hand, and then quickly pulled away before he could squeeze the life out of it. "I need to write a note to Jake." The storekeeper slid a piece of paper and pencil toward her. She quickly wrote a note telling her plans. "Can you see that he gets it?" She handed it back to the man behind the counter.

He nodded. "I'll take care of it."

ও

The wagon proved rough and slow enough to make Hannah grind her teeth. And Jud was talkative. She soon discovered he pretty much carried the conversation on his own, which left her to her thoughts.

She prayed she wasn't on a foolish chase. She prayed the boys were safe. She prayed Jake would find her. If he didn't come, she and the boys—if she found them—would be stranded in Fall River.

"How long will this trip take?" she asked Jud.

"Two hours on a good day."

Hannah gasped. Two hours of rattling around on this hard wooden seat? Would the boys have stayed on the wagon that long? She couldn't imagine they would. Had they even hitched a ride on the other wagon? Somehow convinced they had, she strained to see any sign of little boot tracks in the trail. She scanned the surrounding landscape. *Please, God, if they're out here somewhere, help me find them.*

She thought of how frightened they must be by now. If they were here and not back at the hotel, laughing at the joke they'd played on everyone. In which case, she was on a silly chase. But either way, Jake would come and get her. She could count on his sense of responsibility. As soon as the storeowner delivered the note, she knew Jake would set out.

Two hours later, two relentless hours of having every bone in her body jarred continuously, Jud pointed toward a little cluster of buildings. "Fall River. Hopeful little settlement. Everybody hoping to find gold or free land or maybe just freedom. And you be hoping to find two little boys. Sorry we saw no sign of them along the trail." Jud had soon realized she kept her eyes open for them and had grown as attentive as she to any indication the boys had been this way.

Her bones continued to rattle even after the horses stopped moving. Hannah felt certain she'd rattle for days. She wanted to jump down as easily as Jud had but discovered her limbs didn't share the same idea as her head.

Jud lifted her to the ground. "Frank's wagon's over by the saloon. You want me to go ask him?"

"Would you, please?" She didn't relish trying to get a man out of the saloon so she could talk to him. She followed Jud but waited several feet away while he went in to find Frank. Jud returned with a man as tall and thick as he was.

After introductions, Hannah asked, "Have you seen two little boys who might have been looking for some caves? Is there any chance they hitched a ride on your wagon?"

Frank scratched his head. "You know, it crossed my mind the boxes at the back had been shifted. I put it down to the trail, but now that you mention it, it could have been two boys. Thought I heard a strange noise a time or two." He roared with laughter. "Don't that beat all? Tough little tykes to head off on their own."

"But did you actually see them? Would you know where they might be now?"

Frank shook his head like a big bull. "Can't say's I do. You say they was looking for caves?" At Hannah's nod, he pointed toward the hills. "Guess I'd be looking over there." He pointed out a trail.

Hannah thanked both men, paused to get a long, cold drink at the pump, and then followed the trail. She shivered as a cool wind tugged at her hair. The sky darkened with a threatening storm. *God, help me find the boys.*

She bent to examine a print in the dust. The wind had obliterated much of it, but it seemed to be the right size for one of the boys. She stood, looked around, and saw nothing but trees and black clouds. "Luke, Sammy, are you there? Can you hear me?"

eight

Jake paced the sidewalk for fifteen minutes. It felt like three hours. With a muffled groan, he strode back into the hotel. "You're sure they didn't come back?"

Mother twisted her hankie into a rope. "Jake, don't you think I'd notice? I'm as worried about them as you. I never should have let those two out of my sight. But I thought, how much trouble could they get into in such a short time?"

Jake snorted. "A whole heap. And now Hannah seems to be missing. It's like there's a hole in the middle of the street swallowing them up." Thinking of a hole, he strode into the dining room and looked over the blackened edges. But no one lay on the dirt below. He returned to the lobby.

"I'm sure Hannah's fine," Mother said, her voice thin with worry. "She's a resourceful young woman used to managing on her own."

His mother's words did nothing to make him feel better. He stared out the window, ground around, crossed the dining room, and opened cupboards in the kitchen as if Hannah and the boys hid among the jars and dishes. He strode to Hannah's bedroom door but hesitated. He had no right to intrude into her privacy. But he had to assure himself the room was empty, so he pushed open the door.

He saw a room as neat and tidy as Hannah. A silver-handled brush and mirror lay on a white cloth on the tall dresser, a Bible on the little stand. A patchwork quilt covered the bed.

He could feel the memory of Hannah's presence in the room, but neither Hannah nor the boys were there.

He checked the backyard again, called their names, and discouraged, returned to the hotel. "Mother, I can't wait here. If any of them show up, keep them here, even if you have to hog-tie them."

He plunked his hat on and hurried back out. He stood in the middle of the street and tried to think where to look that he hadn't already looked two or three times. His gaze touched the church at the far end of the street, and he hurried that direction. He quietly pulled the door open, stepped inside to the quiet, made his way to the front, and knelt at the prayer rail.

"God," he whispered, "I need help in finding Luke and Sammy and Hannah. You see them. Show me where they are. Protect them." He leaned his head against his forearms and let his heart open before God. How would he forgive himself if something happened to the little boys who were his responsibility?

And if he couldn't find Hannah? He'd known her such a short time, and yet he couldn't imagine life without her. He tried to think what that meant. Why was Hannah so important to him? It wasn't as if she wanted him to care. But his heart was too troubled to be able to sort out his feelings. He knew only that it was his responsibility to find the three of them and make sure nothing bad happened to them. Again he prayed for God's help.

He heard the door open and scrambled to his feet. But it was only a young boy waving a slip of paper. "Mr. Sperling, my father saw you go into the church and sent me to give you this."

Jake reached the boy in six long strides and snatched the paper and read:

Jake,
  I think I know where the boys are. Remember how Luke wanted to see the caves. There are two wagons headed west today. I think they got on the first and I am getting on the second. I'll find them if they're out there, and we'll wait for you to come for us.

Hannah

Jake scrunched the paper and jammed it in his pocket. At the door he remembered his manners and called, "Thanks."

He ran all the way to the hotel to tell his mother where he was headed and then ran all the way to the corrals to saddle his horse and race through town. He'd gone half a mile when he realized he'd have to settle into a pace meant to last awhile.

Riding gave him time to think about what he'd do when he found Hannah. Once he made sure she was in one piece, he'd scold her for doing something so foolish. Then he'd kiss her and make her promise to give up the hotel and come out to the ranch where he could keep an eye on her and make sure she was safe.

A cold wind bit through his jacket. The sky twisted and churned like a mad bull. It seemed to take forever to get to Fall River. He jumped off his horse and hurried into the low-roofed store. "I'm looking for a woman and two little boys," he called. He didn't realize how loud his voice was until the other two people in the store stared at him, expressions startled. He lowered his voice. "They came in on the supply wagons."

A reed of a man nodded. "Woman came in. Asked about

two boys. Seen her headed thatta way." He pointed to a trail.

"How long ago?" Jake demanded.

The man cocked his head as if looking for the answer someplace just above Jake's right ear. "Can't rightly say. Been busy unloading the wagon. But if I had to guess, I'd say an hour. Maybe two. You ask me, it's not a good day for a woman and young 'uns to be adventuring alone. Storm's a-brewin'."

Jake spun around and headed the direction the man pointed, aware the sky had grown even more ominous in the few minutes he'd been inside.

"Hannah, Sammy, Luke," he roared. The wind tore the words from his mouth.

❧

Hannah shivered against the cold and called the boys again. She didn't look at the sky. She already knew what she didn't want to acknowledge—they were in for a drenching. She pushed into the wind as she staggered up a hill. Her constant prayer had been reduced to a few words repeated over and over. *Help me find them. Help me find them.*

The wind increased. It moaned through the trees and screamed down the hills. The scream had a familiar sound. She stopped and stood motionless, listening hard. Could it be the boys?

She yelled at the top of her voice but knew they'd never hear her if they were yelling, too. She ducked her head into the wind, trying to determine what direction the screams came from. She shifted toward the right, shook her head, shifted left, and then continued another step and another. Were the voices getting clearer or did she only hope for it?

She shivered and took another step toward the sound. *Please, God guide me to them.* The wind shifted, paused, and then renewed itself. But not before Hannah heard the screams. She knew for certain it was the boys and pinpointed the direction. She climbed a knoll and saw them a hundred feet away huddled in a hollow. She lifted her skirts and ran toward them.

Luke saw her first. "Hannah."

Sammy burst into tears.

Hannah reached them, fell on her knees, and pulled them both into her arms. "Thank God you're safe." They clung so tightly she could hardly breathe, but she wasn't about to complain.

Luke pulled away first. "It's my fault," he whispered. "I knew we shouldn't go away, but we wanted to see the caves before we went home."

Hannah backed into the almost-cave until she pressed against the cool earthen wall and pulled the boys to her lap. They were out of the wind and safe.

Sammy snuggled close. "We found this cave. Then we got scared 'cause we didn't know how we'd get home. And then we got cold."

Luke held his little brother's hand. "I prayed just like Mommy said I should. I asked God to forgive me and send Uncle Jake to get us. 'Stead He sent you. I'm glad. Uncle Jake would be mad."

Hannah chuckled. "Uncle Jake is coming to get us."

Luke sat up. His bottom lip trembled. "He'll be mad at us."

"He's worried about you. So is Grandma. I was, too. We couldn't imagine what happened to you. You must promise never to do such a thing again."

"We won't," they chorused.

No doubt they'd learned their lesson. She couldn't imagine how frightened they were when they realized the significance of their little adventure. She held them close, enjoying the warmth of their little bodies.

In an effort to ease their worry about Uncle Jake's reaction, she told them stories of her own childhood. Living in town provided a stark contrast to their lives. She told about games she played with the neighborhood children—Auntie I Over, Kick the Can, and Cops and Robbers. "I loved running down the alleys, trying to keep out of sight of the others." Her father had built her a tall swing in the backyard and given her use of a little shed where she played house with her friends.

"I'm going to ask Daddy to build me a swing," Luke said.

Hannah watched the clouds grow darker and saw the first drops of rain. Where was Jake?

She felt neither fear nor worry. Jake would come. He would never let a person down. His conscience would not allow it. She just had to sit tight, out of the rain and wind, sheltered, and although not comfortably warm, at least not more than slightly cold.

Sammy's eyes drooped, and Luke seemed content to cuddle against her. She shifted to a more comfortable position. Jake might have taken shelter until the storm blew over.

She leaned her head back. It was nice to know she could count on Jake. In the few days she'd known him she'd been impressed with his strength of character and his sense of responsibility. She'd allowed herself to think it once before—she could love this man. She smiled widely. Who was she fooling? Not herself for sure. She'd fallen top over teakettle, flat out in love with him. She would even consider giving up the hotel if he asked her to marry him. The thought stunned her.

"Hannah?" Her name came to her on the wind. She heard it again and realized it wasn't just her gentle thoughts but a voice from outside in the rain.

She edged Sammy to the rocky ground, left Luke at his side, and scrambled to the opening. "Jake. We're here."

He rode into sight, waved, and galloped toward them. He reined in and jumped to the ground. "Hannah," he pulled her into his arms, pressing her cheek against his wet jacket. "Thank God you're safe. All of you." He released her and stepped back. "And here I am getting you all wet."

"I don't mind." She would ride through the storm if it meant being with him.

He ducked into the "cave." "Boys," he yelled, "what do you think you're doing running off like that?"

"Jake, they've learned their lesson."

"I'm sorry, Uncle Jake," Luke said at the same time.

And Sammy, startled awake, began to bawl at the top of his voice.

Jake took a step backward and scrubbed his hand over his wet face. "I kind of turned the peace upside down."

"Yes, you did."

"Aww. Luke, Sammy, I was so worried about you." He shrugged out of his wet jacket and held out his arms to the boys. They threw themselves into his embrace and hung on. Not releasing them, he scooted around and settled down. "We might as well sit this storm out. Room for you here." He tipped his head to one side. "We'll keep warm and dry together."

Hannah settled in beside him and took Sammy on her lap.

Jake spoke softly. "I was worried when I couldn't find you."

Hannah knew he meant her, and she smiled all the way to the bottom of her heart. "The wagon wouldn't wait. I felt I had to take advantage of the ride."

"Of course it never crossed your mind to come to me and ask for help."

She blinked. "I sent you a message. I knew you'd come." Her voice grew round with love for this man. He'd admitted his concern. But did it go any further?

"I would have preferred for you to come and inform me and let me be the one to go into the wilds to find them." He kept his voice soft because of the sleeping boys, but there was no disguising the iron behind his words.

"I did what I thought best. Surely you understand." She silently pleaded with him to see that she did what she had to. "I had to make a decision, and I did."

Luke's head tipped forward, and he snored softly. Jake shifted the child so his head rested on Jake's arm.

"You're far too independent."

She didn't know how to respond. Did he mean it as a compliment or a criticism? She hoped the former, but it was hard to tell as he kept his voice soft for the sake of the boys.

He shifted. "The rain is letting up. As soon as it quits, we'll walk back to Fall River. I'll see if I can borrow a wagon or buggy to get us back to Quinten. After I turn this pair over to my mother, you and I will have a talk."

That sounded just fine to her. There were so many things she wanted to tell him. Not that she planned to blurt out the truth about falling in love with him. But she was certainly open to any suggestion on his part. She sighed. Courtship and marriage sounded mighty appealing.

The rain stopped and the sun came out. Moisture sparkled on every surface. They wakened the boys. Jake put them on the horse, and he and Hannah led the way back to Fall River.

Hannah waited with the boys in the little store, gratefully accepting the offer of tea and sandwiches as Jake went to find a conveyance back. She hoped it wouldn't be one of the freight wagons. But in the end, that's exactly what they rode as Jud gave them a ride back to town. Jake sat on the hard seat beside Jud and listened to the man's stories while Hannah sat in the back with the boys.

❧

Dark filled the sky long before they returned to the hotel. Hannah watched Mrs. Sperling break into tears as she saw them all safe. "I've been beside myself with worry," she said.

Jake led his mother inside and settled her on the sofa. The little boys trailed in and climbed up on either side of her, and she held them close, tears filling her eyes. "Thank you." She included Hannah in her look.

"I'm going to find something for us to eat." Jake hurried out the door.

Hannah sat and listened to the boys retelling their adventure. Luke again promised he would never be so naughty in the future.

Mrs. Sperling hugged the boys. "What you did was wrong, but I'm just glad you're both safe. And you, too, Hannah."

Jake returned bearing plates of food. A young man who worked in one of the restaurants carried more plates, and they settled in for a good feast.

Hannah didn't expect to be able to eat. Her insides felt jittery as she waited for the chance to talk to Jake alone. Yet her appetite took over. Even the little boys, so tired they could barely keep their faces out of their plates, ate with gusto.

Sammy finally caved in, and Jake pulled his plate away before the child's face hit the table. "I'll help you get them into bed," he told his mother. He scooped Sammy up and carried him up the stairs while Mrs. Sperling followed, half dragging Luke.

Hannah piled the plates and left them to be picked up. She wandered around the lobby. She paused to look out at the sleeping street.

When she heard Jake's footsteps on the stairs, she didn't immediately turn. Her heart felt like it had shrunk with trepidation and then ballooned with expectation. Would he say what she wanted him to? Give some indication that his feelings mirrored hers? Give her a reason to reconsider her need to fix this hotel?

"Can we talk now?" Jake asked, and she turned toward his gentle voice. She saw uncertain guardedness in his eyes. She smiled, hoping he'd see the longing and love she felt, then took the chair he indicated. He sat facing her and gave her a long look. She hoped to see her feelings reflected in his gaze, but what she saw didn't feel right. But then she understood his confusion. She hadn't even hinted at how she felt. She leaned forward in anticipation, encouraging him to reveal his feelings. "Yes?"

"Hannah, I've decided you should come to the ranch with us."

She blinked once and nodded. Was this Jake's idea of an invitation? He often chose the most direct way of saying something.

He continued. "I'll be able to keep an eye on you. It's the only way I can make sure you don't rush off and do something stupid and foolish like you did today."

"Stupid? Foolish? I found the boys. Kept them safe until you arrived."

"What you did was almost as irresponsible as the boys. No one knew where you were. And did you ever think what the wagon driver could have done?"

Her anticipation curled into anger. "It wasn't a thoughtless risk. I knew Jud wouldn't hurt me. I can read character pretty well, you know." Only she wondered if she could. She'd been expecting Jake to say something much different.

"I've made up my mind," he said. "You will accompany us to the ranch. You get along well with Mother. You can help her out, keep her company."

"You've made up your mind?" She could barely get the words past the disappointment clawing at her throat. "In case you've forgotten, I have a hotel to run."

"It's a dead horse. About time you put it out of its misery and forgot the whole thing. If you're concerned about money, I'll pay you to be Mother's companion."

She jumped to her feet, forcing him to tip his head back to look at her. "Jake Sperling, I will not be ordered around by anyone. I will not be sold or bought or controlled. I will only be accepted for what I am. I don't need taking care of, as you seem to think. And I will run this hotel." She raced across the dining room, barely avoiding the hole, and into her bedroom, slamming the door loudly enough to inform Jake the conversation was over.

She sank to the edge of the bed and moaned. How could she be so blind, so stupid? Jake didn't think of her with love in his heart; he saw her only as another responsibility. Someone to order about. She dashed away tears stinging her eyes and stared straight ahead, right at the chiffonier. She thought of her father's pocket watch and groaned. How could she have forgotten her goal—to honor her father's memory by living up to his expectations of her?

nine

Jake helped his mother into the buggy and ordered the boys to settle down. He'd had glimpses of Hannah in the kitchen as they prepared to leave, but she seemed determined to avoid him. Stubborn, headstrong, and far too independent, she'd made it plain he had no choice but to leave her here on her own. Even though it grated against his nature.

He wondered if she'd avoid him until they left, but she stepped out, her head high, smiling at the boys and his mother, avoiding his gaze. Yes, it annoyed him. Even hurt a little. He knew he'd made her angry last night. But sooner or later she would see he was right. She didn't belong here alone.

"I'll miss you," she told the boys, ruffling their hair. They each hugged her and promised to come see her again.

"I want you to come visit us at the ranch next Sunday," his mother said as she and Hannah hugged. "You will, won't you?"

"Yeah," the boys screamed.

Hannah hesitated. "I have no means of transportation."

"Jake will come and get you, won't you, Jake?"

Jake knew he was trapped. He couldn't refuse his mother. Besides, maybe Hannah refused to obey him because she had no idea what the ranch was like. He'd never thought of that. "Sure, I'll come and get you." She'd soon agree when she saw how beautiful it was.

"Why not make it Saturday so she can have a long visit?" Mother asked.

"Saturday, then? If you can tear yourself away from the hotel."

Hannah met his gaze then with her own silent challenge. "Saturday evening is fine."

He didn't miss the emphasis on *evening*.

"Mort will be here."

❧

It had been only five days, Jake reminded himself, as he drove into Quinten. Five days in which he thought of Hannah off and on. Like about a thousand times a day. He had no trouble picturing her waiting for him when he strode into the house, sitting across from him at the hand-hewn table, waving as he rode from the yard to check on the cows. She'd never been in his house or stood on his veranda or seen the hills of his ranch, yet in his thoughts she fit right in as though his world had been waiting all his life for her.

He pulled to a stop in front of the Sunshine Hotel and jumped off to go in search of Hannah. He found her in the lobby, her bag at her feet. He skidded to a halt and twisted his hat in his hands. She was even more beautiful than he remembered and didn't look any worse for wear, though he expected she had worked hard since he'd seen her, trying to prove she could do as well as a man. And although her eyes were guarded, he couldn't keep from grinning his pleasure.

She smiled uncertainly, answering his greeting softly.

"You're ready. Good." He crossed to her side, grabbed the bag, and held out his elbow to guide her. "Mother and the boys are eager to see you again, and Audrey is dying to meet you." He noticed the dining door had been boarded over with fresh lumber. He could smell the newness of it.

He waited until she sat beside him on the wagon before he

asked her the questions burning in his mind. "Did you get the place open?"

"I have four rooms rented out already. No one has complained about the lack of a dining room." She gave a little laugh. "It feels good to finally be doing business."

He wanted to point out she didn't need to work. She could let someone else take care of her. She didn't have to prove anything. He stuffed back his arguments, knowing she wouldn't listen, moreover, would likely get angry if he voiced them and maybe refuse to accompany him. Then he'd have to face his mother's displeasure and Audrey's endless questions. Instead, he turned to the obvious. "Did you fix the floor in the dining room?"

"Not yet."

"Seems you'll have to do it one of these days. Wasn't it on the warning from the town council?"

"You know it was." Her voice sounded crisp, informing him she didn't care for his questions. "I'm waiting until I have enough money; then I'll hire some men to fix it."

He chuckled. "I kind of figured you'd be measuring and sawing it yourself."

"I probably could, but I prefer to get someone who knows how to fix the floor so it isn't a danger to my guests."

He didn't know how to respond. Her answers never satisfied him. He wanted her to admit defeat and give up the hotel. He believed she'd be singing another tune after visiting the ranch and experiencing a taste of life lived where a man was a man. He stopped himself before he finished the saying. *And a woman was a woman.*

He always thought of a woman as his father had taught him to see her. Someone to take care of. Weaker than a man. Hannah refused to fit into that description. She insisted she didn't need or want to be taken care of. What would it take to change her mind? His only answer—learning to love the ranch. Intent on making that happen, he turned to point out things along the trail. She seemed interested as he identified the trees and birds.

As they approached his land, he made sure she noticed its beauties. He drew to a halt near a copse of trees. "I remember finding a calf there, and when I got down to help the little guy, I found a baby rabbit." He flicked the reins and moved on, pointing out a tall tree. "Every year a pair of hawks nest there. Have you ever seen a young hawk try out its wings for the first time?"

"Can't say I have."

"It's a wondrous sight."

She chuckled. "You have a special connection to the land."

He grew quiet. His intention had been to make her see the beauties of the ranch, not how much he loved the place. But the visit had just begun. By the time she'd seen the sunset flare across the sky, felt the sun on her face in the morning, heard the coyotes singing at night, walked along the edge of a hill where she could see forever and a day. . .

&

Hannah had given herself a serious talk every day of the past week and a triple dose of caution today as she prepared for her trip to the ranch. This visit was a chance to see his mother and the two little boys and meet Audrey. Jake had fetched her to please his mother. She'd almost allowed herself to fall in love with him only to discover he saw her as yet another of his many responsibilities. It made her feel burdensome.

Yet as she listened to the love and pride in his voice as he extolled the beauties of his ranch, she didn't know whether to be envious of the land or angry he reserved his affection for nothing more than rock and dirt, plants and animals. But one thing she knew for sure—she wished he would look at her with half the love she saw glowing in his eyes as he pointed out things.

When he indicated a herd of antelope racing across a field, she had to sit on her hands to keep from grabbing his arm and pulling his attention to her. She wanted him to see her. Not as a responsibility but as a person equal to him with different strengths and abilities, just as capable of making choices and decisions.

She turned around to look away from him to the passing scenery. Why did she torture herself with impossible wishes especially when she had what she wanted back in Quinten? A hotel of her own. No one to tell her who she should be. So what if she was alone? It was better than being someone's responsibility.

Jake pulled the buggy to a halt and pointed. "There it is."

"So many buildings." A big hip-roofed barn, several scattered outbuildings she couldn't guess the use of, a long, low building that Jake said was the bunkhouse for the men, but the house dominated the scene. Two stories with balconies outside the upstairs windows and a veranda on the west side of the first floor. Made of weathered logs, large enough to be impressive, it looked solid enough to defy anything the elements might send.

"There's the church." He directed her gaze past the house, past the barn, past the clustered outbuildings to a narrow, steep-roofed log structure tucked against the trees on one side just as he'd said. "We'll worship there tomorrow."

"I look forward to it." More than she cared to admit. All her self-admonition, all her reminders of how proud her father would be were but whispers with this man at her side. Even though she knew he did not return her feelings, she could not deny her love for him. Spending time with him would be a pleasure laced with aching disappointment.

Jake groaned, "The boys have seen you."

Hannah chuckled. The pair bounced up and down on the veranda. Even from this distance she could hear them screaming her name.

Jake flicked the reins, and they made their way to the house. She waited for Jake to help her down. He remained at her side as the boys launched themselves at her. Only Jake's steadying arm across her back kept her on her feet.

She darted him a grateful look. She thought his gaze would be on the boys, but he stared at her, his eyes almost black and so bottomless she felt dizzy. She wanted to turn into his arms, but two bodies wrapped around her legs made it impossible. She pulled away, the world stopped spinning, and she bent to pull Sammy and Luke into a tight hug.

Mrs. Sperling joined them and waited for Hannah to untangle herself from the boys. Laughing at the joyous greeting, Hannah reached for Mrs. Sperling's outstretched hands.

"I'm so glad you're here, my dear," the older woman said. She then told the boys, "Better let her go so we can go inside." The boys raced ahead, and Mrs. Sperling took Hannah's hand and pulled it through her arm. "Audrey is eager to meet you."

Hannah glanced back and saw Jake still watching her, looking as if he wanted to say something. She hesitated. She couldn't keep from hoping he wanted to convince her things could be different between them. She'd accept anything as a starting spot. Anything but responsibility. But his expression changed, grew harder, determined even, and he swung back to the buggy seat and drove away.

Inside, a young woman bounced toward her and screamed. "You're Hannah. I've heard so much about you. I'm Audrey. I understand you rescued my two little imps. Thank you. I do my best to keep them out of trouble, but they still find it."

Hannah smiled and held her breath waiting for Audrey to run out of steam. It was obvious where the boys got their rambunctiousness.

Hannah looked around the room—she didn't know if she should call it a living room or a lobby. It rose two stories to the log ceiling. A balcony ran along three sides on the second level. Beyond the rails she saw doors she guessed opened to bedrooms.

She lowered her gaze to the huge windows at the far end of this room and gasped. Her heart felt ready to explode at the sweeping view of hills and trees. Slowly she brought her gaze back inside to the furnishings. A sideboard big enough to hide in. Three leather sofas formed a square with one open side. A bookcase eight feet high filled with books and collectibles—a globe of the world, a carving that looked to be from some Indian tribe, a perfectly round rock, and a china statue of a young woman with her skirts flared at her ankles.

As she looked around, the family slowly moved her across the floor to a large dining room featuring a long table of polished split logs. She brushed her fingers over it. Smooth as silk.

"Have a seat, dear," Mrs. Sperling said.

Hannah chose the closest chair. Sammy and Luke climbed up on either side of her. Mrs. Sperling sat at the end, and Audrey hurried around to sit opposite Hannah. A woman hustled in through the swinging door. Hannah caught a glimpse of a big kitchen; then Mrs. Sperling demanded her attention.

"Hannah, this is my dear friend and the one who keeps our household running, Sarie."

The big-framed woman with a mop of gray curls leaned over and hugged Hannah. "Any friend of this family's is a friend of mine."

A few minutes later, Hannah met Audrey's husband, Harvey, who had a bullhorn of a voice.

Sarie brought tea and a huge tray of cakes and cookies.

Hannah enjoyed meeting Audrey and Harvey and seeing again Mrs. Sperling and the boys, but she kept hoping Jake would join them. He finally did, and suddenly she felt awkward in his presence and wished he would leave.

She let the conversation flow around her, adding replies when required, but she felt like a spectator. Several times she felt Jake's gaze on her, but when she met his eyes, he jerked away. She almost sighed with relief when Audrey said it was time to put the boys to bed and took her family home. Mrs. Sperling turned to Hannah. "I'll show you to your room."

She rose to follow the older woman to the stairs then paused. "Good night, Jake."

He glanced up from his study of his teacup. "Good night, Hannah."

Their eyes locked. His burned through every argument, every reasonable defense she'd built. She felt its power right to the bottom of her heart and knew a moment of panic followed swiftly by shame. She was a strong, independent woman, but God forgive her, she knew if at that moment he'd asked her to give up everything she had and was and wanted, she gladly would have done it.

But he didn't ask. He wouldn't. Oh, he might order her to do certain things, but she would never allow herself to be ordered around. She had far too much spunk for that. She had an independent spirit.

She was the first to pull away from the fire of their gaze. With a nod she left the room and followed Mrs. Sperling to the second floor.

"I hope you'll be comfortable."

Hannah chuckled at the idea of anyone being anything but comfortable in this house. "It's a beautiful room."

"I put out a selection of books if you want to read. But don't feel you have to stay in your room. We rise early so I'm going to bed now, but if you want to go downstairs and sit by the fire, please do."

"I think I'll go to bed and read. Thank you." After Mrs. Sperling left, Hannah glanced through the titles of the books and chose one. But she didn't read. She went to the windows and looked out.

The ranch was beautiful. The house itself, spectacular, as big as her hotel with a warmer feel. It was a home, a home belonging to the ranch as much as to the family. She closed her eyes. She could almost feel the solidness of the place. She breathed deeply and opened her eyes.

The balcony outside her room looked so inviting, she slipped out. She shivered in the cool evening air and let the peace of her surroundings fill her. She could almost imagine belonging here. The sound of boots crunching on the ground below and the bulky shape she recognized as Jake sent her back against the wall.

How could she be so foolish to love a man who didn't love

her back? She wondered if he knew how to love without being in charge. She slipped inside and prepared for bed then opened the book she'd chosen and forced herself to read the words.

❧

Hannah sat at the table with Jake, Mrs. Sperling, Audrey, her family, and Pastor Rawson. Last night she'd finally fallen asleep once she'd made her mind up to avoid being alone with Jake. How else was she to make it through Sunday without her emotions getting all knotted up?

So far she'd been successful. Jake hadn't joined them at breakfast. His mother said he'd gone to speak with some of the crew, so Hannah enjoyed a visit with Mrs. Sperling.

She managed to get Luke and Sammy on either side of her at the church. Audrey and Harvey had followed her into the pew, leaving no room for Jake. He sat behind them.

Hannah caught glimpses of him as they stood to sing. She continued to be aware of him and wondered if she would ever not feel his presence, whether he stood close or rode miles away.

It had been a beautiful service in a beautiful building, and she tried not to picture herself coming down the aisle with the light catching the threads of a shimmering veil. She'd had to close her eyes and pray for strength to keep herself from seeing Jake in a black suit waiting for her at the front.

She concentrated hard on the sermon. She knew it had been sent straight from God's heart to hers when Pastor Rawson read the text. "The spirit indeed is willing but the flesh is weak." As Pastor Rawson talked about how flesh warred against spirit, desiring things that were temporary, tempting the believer to settle for momentary pleasure, Hannah vowed to stick to her principles. She would keep the vow she'd made to her father, a vow given at his graveside. Even though he hadn't heard it, she had meant it. She'd promised to live up to his expectations. She would not compromise her independence. Not for the joy of living on this ranch. Not for the sight of Jake every day. Not for the hope his feelings would grow into love. Unless he accepted her as she wanted, there was no place for her here.

Pastor Rawson accompanied them home for supper, as apparently was his custom. Audrey, Harvey, and the boys joined them, too, so the conversation jumped from one topic to another. Audrey tried to keep the boys quiet, but after Sammy spilled his cake on the floor and Luke tipped over his third glass of milk, Audrey stood. "I think it's time to take this pair home and let them run off steam. Boys, say good-bye to Hannah."

Hannah hugged the pair, received two sticky kisses, and said good-bye to Audrey and Harvey.

As Sarie cleaned away the dishes, Mrs. Sperling glanced at Jake. "I'd like to speak to the pastor alone."

Hannah pushed back her chair. "I'll go up to my room and read."

"Nonsense," Mrs. Sperling said. "It's far too pleasant an evening to be cooped up indoors. Jake, take her for a walk."

"My pleasure." Jake slowly got to his feet, his gaze never leaving Hannah's face. She tried to look away, to pretend she didn't see the promise in his eyes. She couldn't any more than she could pull the stars from the sky or deflect the sun from its journey from east to west. Nor did she want to. She wanted the fulfillment of the promise in his rich brown eyes—a look, she felt certain, was full of love.

They walked side by side, talking of everything and nothing— the color of the sky, the sound of the breeze, the boys' mischief, the beauty of their surroundings. They passed the church and sat on a fallen tree.

"How do you like my ranch?" Jake asked.

"It's beautiful."

"Does it live up to your expectations?"

"It exceeds them. I never could have imagined a place could seem to be so much a part of the land, like one exists for the other." She ducked her head. "Now I'm being silly."

He took her hand. "I don't think so. In fact, you've perfectly expressed what I have always felt but didn't have words for. I'm glad you like it. It's important you do."

She kept her head down, but her heart had to know if his eyes would give a clue as to what he meant. Slowly, her breath clinging motionless to her ribs, she lifted her face and met his eyes. He looked uncertain as if he waited for her to indicate something. "Why?" she whispered.

He caught a strand of hair the breeze had pulled loose, tucked it behind her ear, and trailed his finger down her cheek. " 'Cause I want you to be happy here."

Happy? Knowing he was about to express his love, she knew happiness like she'd never known. Like the softness of rabbit fur, the scent of a perfect rose, and the sight of a newborn baby all rolled up into one and dropped into her heart. "I could be very happy here."

He dropped his hand to slap his thigh. "Then it's settled. You'll get rid of the hotel and move out here."

"Why?"

"Why what?"

"Why should I move out here?" If he would only hint he had some feelings toward her, but his expression grew hard, distant.

"Seems to me it's pretty clear. You need to be out here where I can make sure you're safe."

Her thoughts were dying butterflies falling to the ground. She rose and quietly headed back to the house.

He followed and grabbed her elbow, forcing her to stop and face him. "I thought you liked the ranch. Didn't you say you could be happy here?"

She nodded. "I could under the right circumstances. But being your servant is not one of them."

"You're far too independent."

She shook her head sadly. "I don't think so, but thank you for reminding me of what's important."

"I suppose you're going to say your independence is more important than your safety."

"I wasn't, because I would never put my personal safety at risk." But she'd put her emotions at risk by allowing herself to think Jake might actually care for her as more than a responsibility. "First, let me be very clear on one thing. You have no right or reason to feel responsible for me. And second, I would be dishonoring my father's memory if I sacrificed my independence in order to be taken care of as you suggest." Pulling herself from his grasp, she returned to the house, found Pastor Rawson preparing to return to town, and asked if she might ride with him.

ten

Next morning, Jake headed for the hills to check on his cows. He wanted space to think. And he didn't need to be around his family, inflicting his bad mood on them.

What was wrong with Hannah? She said she liked the ranch. She had no reason to lie, so it must be true. Yet she refused to do the sensible thing and move here.

His stomach knotted and twisted and turned sour as he thought of her remaining in town. Unless she could be persuaded to visit again, he'd have to go to town to see her, and how often could he do that? Not often enough to satisfy the emptiness inside him at the thought of not seeing her for weeks on end. He guessed every day wouldn't be enough. Something about that gal got under his skin and refused to let go. In a way he sort of liked. No, the idea of seeing her at most once a week, knowing she was in town trying to fix and run that hotel on her own, just sliced along his nerves like a sliver under his fingernail.

The hotel was the cause of this trouble between them. And it was all tied up to something she seemed to think her father expected of her. None of which made a lick of sense. He figured any man would see the predicament Hannah had gotten herself into and find a way to get her out. But Hannah was stuck with nothing but memories of what she thought her father wanted, and she couldn't seem to pull away from them. She'd said it often enough that he didn't have any trouble recalling what she thought her father expected of her—get the hotel fixed up and opened.

He sat on his horse, staring at the rolling hills he loved. The hotel kept Hannah from his side.

She would never admit defeat, because she somehow had it figured her father would be disappointed in her if she did. So the way to solve the problem was to help her get the hotel fixed up so she could walk away without feeling she'd disappointed her father.

And he knew exactly how to do it.

He reined his horse around and galloped back to the ranch. Only Zeke answered his call.

"The others are out checking the cows like you said," he replied in answer to Jake's demand to know where everyone had disappeared to.

"Go find half a dozen of them. I've got something in town needs doing."

Two hours later he sent Zeke and six of his outfit to town with instructions to fix the hole in the dining room floor of the hotel. "Get lumber at the hardware store. Do it right. I want it ready to use when you're done." He saw them on their way then rode over to the house to inform his mother he was on his way to town.

"Wait," she called, "I want you to pick up a few things."

"Mother, you were just in town." He wanted to see the look on Hannah's face when his crew showed up to fix the dining room. He could well imagine her surprise, her confusion, and then her delight at getting this job done before the deadline set by the mayor and his cronies.

"I need some more thread. Just wait while I get you a sample of cloth so Mrs. Johnson can match it."

He drummed his fingers on the banister as he waited for her to run upstairs. A few minutes later, she returned. "Audrey's just coming over the hill. Let me see if she needs anything."

"Mother, I'm in a hurry."

"What's a minute or two?" Ignoring his protests, she hurried out the back door to meet Audrey. Sammy and Luke screamed a greeting to their grandmother.

Jake twisted his hat and ground his teeth. He wanted to be there when the boys arrived with the load of lumber.

Mother returned. "She'd like you to pick up—never mind, I'll write it down."

Jake fumed as she found a piece of paper then had to sharpen the pencil, but finally he was on his way, galloping his mount to make up for lost time.

He didn't catch them by the time he slowed for Quinten's main street. As he approached the hotel, he saw the men still mounted, Zeke still seated in the wagon. Hannah stood on the sidewalk, her arms crossed over her chest. He'd missed seeing her surprise.

He reined in, dropped to the ground, wrapped the reins twice around the hitching post, and clattered to her side. "Are you surprised?" he asked.

She faced him. "Do I look surprised?"

His smile faded, his shoulders tensed as he took a good look at her. Her eyes flashed. Her mouth pulled down at the corners. He hoped he was mistaken, but she looked angry. He turned to his crew. "What are you waiting for? Let's get this done."

The men shifted and looked uncomfortable.

"What's going on here?"

"They might as well go back to the ranch. I've told them

I don't need their help."

No one moved. Jake felt the heat of Hannah's gaze and saw the awkwardness of his men.

Hannah waved her hand dismissively. "You can leave now."

The men waited for his order.

"Jake." Her voice was deceptively soft. "Tell them to leave."

He scratched his neck. "I thought my crew could. . ."

She pushed her face closer to his. He felt her hot breath, caught a glimpse of hazel fire in her eyes before he shifted his gaze to avoid looking at her. "Jake, I will hire my own crew when I'm ready." She made an explosive sound, turned, and steamed into the hotel.

Jake sighed. "Boys, you might as well go on home. She's too stubborn to change her mind."

Looking relieved, they rode away.

Jake stood outside the door for a minute, trying to make sense of the whole thing, finally admitted there was no sense to be made, and pushed inside. "Hannah, you said you needed some men to fix the floor."

She spun around to face him.

He didn't need the sight in both eyes to see she was still angry.

"How dare you presume to take over my responsibilities!" Her voice could have cut steel.

"I—"

"What makes you so certain I can't manage on my own? How dare you treat me like you do your family!"

"I—" But whatever reason or argument he might have dredged up never got a chance.

"Why do you have to fix everyone?" She took a step closer. "Can't you see not everyone needs fixing or taking care of?"

She took two more steps until her shoes were an inch from the tips of his boots.

He stifled an urge to back away from her anger.

"Have you ever tried just accepting people? Allowing them to make their own choices. Giving them the freedom to make mistakes. Why do you have to be responsible for everything? Why do you think if people make a mistake you've failed? Jake, did you ever think that people—your family—would like to be accepted as they are with their flaws and failings, dreams and expectations. And yes, even be allowed a little independence." She breathed so hard, he wondered if a person could get wind-broken.

Then she threw her arms in the air. "Oh, what's the use?" She stomped toward the dining room, apparently remembered the door had been boarded off, and with an angry mutter, shifted directions and headed for the stairs. "If you don't mind, I have work to do."

"Hannah, wait."

She paused and slowly turned. Her anger had calmed and was replaced with resignation. "What?"

"I—" How could he hope for her to understand his intention had been so much more honorable than she assessed it? Wasn't it? "I only wanted to help."

She shook her head. "No, you wanted to be responsible for me. You can't. I am responsible for me. It's not a job that requires two people." Slowly she climbed the stairs and disappeared down the hall.

Jake stared after her for a long time then rode away as fast as he'd made the trip into town.

❧

Hannah sank to the edge of her bed and stared blindly across the room. She'd been holding on to a useless hope, thinking one day Jake would stop trying to control her and learn to love and accept her.

But he'd made it plain as household dust he didn't think she could manage on her own. He didn't see her as an equal, someone who could make decisions and handle challenges using her own resources.

He was right about one thing, though, she had to get the dining room floor fixed in less than a week in order to avoid further fines and run the chance of having the "safety inspector" shut her down. She'd been hoping for more money. But renting three or four rooms at a time, from which she had to pay Mort, buy wallpaper and paint, and purchase food for herself—it all ate away at the little bit of income she'd generated.

She picked up her Bible and opened it but didn't read. Instead, she prayed. *God, You have created me. You have given me opportunities. Long ago, when I first trusted You, it was because of Your promise to provide for my needs. I know You love me with an unsearchable love. Nothing is too hard for You. Show me how to meet this challenge.*

She sat quietly, waiting for God to reveal His will. Her gaze rested on the chiffonier. Her thoughts went to the black case inside the drawer and her father's pocket watch. She wondered what it was worth.

No, Lord. I can't sell it. It's the only thing I have left of my father's belongings.

What would her father want? For her to succeed at this venture? He certainly would. He would encourage her to sell the watch if necessary. She hated to part with it, but she needed the money.

Two tears dripped down her cheeks. She dashed them away.

She would do whatever she had to do. Still she hesitated. Was she desperate enough to sell her most precious belonging?

It was that or face defeat. Her father would be disappointed if she didn't do her best.

She pushed to her feet, took the case from the drawer, and headed down the street. She'd never visited Stephen's Jewelers, but now she stepped into the shop filled with glass-fronted display shelves.

A few minutes later she emerged with more money than she'd anticipated and crossed the street to the hardware store, where she arranged for a man to measure the hole and supply materials to repair it.

૱

A month later, Hannah wandered through the hotel. The dining room floor was finished—the new boards painted mahogany brown to match the old floor. She'd rescued a maroon rug from the storeroom and put it in the center of the room and placed tables and chairs around in a pleasing arrangement that left room for serving and provided a bit of privacy. White tablecloths and candlesticks provided the touch of elegance she wanted. She'd hired a cook and helpers to operate the dining room.

She paused in the lobby, pleased with the new green-apple paint on the wall beside the door and the new wallpaper behind the desk—decorated with cabbage roses. She climbed the stairs and checked each room. She now had a young girl to help clean. All eight rooms were usable and were often full.

The hotel had been successfully reopened. Not even Mayor Stokes or Mr. Bertch could find fault. She returned to the main floor.

Thelma, the cook, beckoned for her attention. "Did you

want to serve biscuits tonight?"

Hannah reviewed the menu with her. She'd never realized how much work it involved to plan a selection of three meals a day, day after day.

She and Thelma managed to plan several days ahead. Hannah made notes of the supplies needed. "I'll order these this afternoon. But I want to do some mending first." It amazed her how much damage her guests did to the sheets and pillowcases. Every week the mending pile grew.

Betty, one of the girls who worked in the dining room, stopped her halfway across the kitchen. "Hannah, I can't work tonight. My mother's sick and needs help with the younger ones."

"Of course. I'll find someone else." She mentally added it to the list of things to be done this afternoon.

Thelma found her again a few minutes later to inform her the butcher hadn't delivered enough meat for their planned menu, and Hannah promised to take care of it.

She barely got settled in a corner of her bedroom and threaded a needle before several other things required her attention. By then the morning had fled away on invisible wings and she had to abandon plans for mending.

She spent the afternoon taking care of errands, managed to persuade Mr. Mack to supply the promised meat, and had to make a few adjustments on her list because Johnson's was out of things. It would mean more planning in order to create the menu. She raced to the telegraph office to send an order for more supplies to be shipped on the train and remembered she didn't have anyone to take Betty's place. She stopped at several houses to ask for someone to work. No one was available, and finally, accepting defeat, she hurried back to the hotel. She had no choice but to help in the dining room and hope Mort would watch the front desk for her.

By the time she made her weary way to her bedroom, she ached from head to toe and a pain had developed in her left leg. She sank to the edge of the bed and buried her head in her hands. She had what she wanted—her business doing well and her independence. So why didn't it feel better?

It wasn't that she minded the work. It kept her from thinking of Jake too often. She hadn't seen him since he'd tried to fix the floor for her. But she missed him with an ache that never let up. It relented only momentarily when her mind was occupied with other things but grew worse at bedtime. How long would it take for her to be able to sit in the quiet of her own room without feeling so alone?

She thought of Mrs. Sperling and smiled. Had the woman learned not to fake headaches and faints? Did she realize her real ones seemed less dramatic when she faked such wonderful false ones?

And Sammy and Luke. Did they miss her? Would she ever again have the pleasure of exploring with them? She supposed the Sperlings would come to town again, and if Mrs. Sperling had her way, they'd stay in Hannah's hotel. But when would such an occasion arise? Probably not until Christmas or even next fall when the cattle were again driven to the rail yard.

Scattered visits were not what she wanted. And playing with Sammy and Luke, visiting Mrs. Sperling, and getting to know Audrey and Harvey better were not what she wanted, either.

What she wanted was Jake. Nothing more. Nothing less.

The hotel might have provided her with independence, but at what price? Why did it feel as if she'd sold herself to a hard taskmaster? Would it be any worse to let Jake order her around? Take care of her?

But she'd promised her father. He'd always valued her independence.

She sighed. What did she want?

The answer was easy. She'd said it to Jake several times. She wanted acceptance.

God accepted her just as she was. Jake's family accepted her.

She jerked up straight and stared ahead. "Oh, Daddy, how could I have been so blind?" she whispered. "It wasn't my independence you valued. It was me."

Perhaps, if she gave him another chance, Jake would learn to accept her as well. Not as a responsibility but as an equal. She chuckled softly. Now that was a goal worth working for.

She prayed for a long time, wanting to be sure the step she planned wasn't simply a reaction to a hard day. She searched the scriptures for guidance. When she read Ephesians, chapter two, verses eight and nine, "For by grace are ye saved through faith; and that not of yourselves: it is the gift of God: not of works, lest any man should boast," she knew she'd found her answer. God didn't need her to prove anything. Nor did she need to prove who she was to Jake.

She laughed. Maybe taking care of people was Jake's way of showing love. She could live with that as long as he could accept her as an equal.

She retrieved paper, pen, and ink from a drawer and wrote a letter to her grandparents. She'd mail it in the morning. And then wait to hear back.

eleven

Jake picked himself off the ground and dusted his clothes.

"He's too much for you, huh, Boss?" Zeke kept all expression from his face and his voice flat, but Jake knew the men got a degree of pleasure out of seeing the wild horse toss him in the dirt. Probably figured it was fair payback for the way he'd driven them the last few weeks.

They'd ridden to the farthest corners of the ranch, searching every gully, every copse of trees, every bluff to make sure all the cows had been gathered in. They'd spent many a night camping out.

Usually a night under the stars mellowed Jake out like nothing else. But he rose early every morning, itching for something he couldn't scratch. He'd rouse the men and head out on another hard ride for some obscure reason.

Trouble was, no matter how hard he drove himself, it did nothing to ease his frustration. No matter how hard he worked, how fast he rode, how many nights he spent out under the stars, he couldn't escape the accusations Hannah had flung at him. Nor could he stop dreaming of her, thinking he saw her at odd moments, wishing she were close by.

Three days ago, he'd decided they'd buy a bunch of wild horses from a trader to the west. It had been a challenge to trail them home, and Jake had accepted no slacking from any of the men. "I paid good bucks for this bunch of knot heads, and every one of them is going to be driven into the corrals and broke."

159

"You hiring someone to break 'em?" Zeke asked.

"I'll do it."

"Yes, Boss."

But the first bronc proved to be difficult. It took all afternoon, but finally Jake managed to stay on the animal and prove who was boss.

He limped into the house for supper. He washed up and strode into the dining room. The table was set, but neither his mother nor Sarie was around. He followed the sound of their voices across the living room to the room his father had used as an office. Jake had never been able to persuade himself to use it. Instead, he'd put a desk in his bedroom where he kept the ranch records.

He ground to a halt and stared at his mother up a ladder holding a piece of fabric to the window. Sarie stood at the other side of the window holding the end of the fabric. "Mother, what do you think you're doing? Get off that ladder before you fall."

His mother shot him a startled look then turned back to Sarie. "It's perfect. What do you think?"

"Sure will freshen up the place."

"Mother." Jake strode across the room, intending to lift her from the ladder.

She waved him away. "In a minute."

"Mother, I insist you get down before you fall."

She finally faced him. Not that he much cared for the gleam in her eye. "You insist? You think you can order me around like I'm one of the hands? Last time I checked, I'm a grown woman in charge of all my faculties. I will decide when I'm done here." And she turned back to pinning the fabric.

He backed off. "What are you doing in here anyway? No one comes in this room."

"It's a lovely room. I'm tired of it being wasted. If you don't want to use it as an office, I'm going to fix it up as a small sitting room. I thought I'd put my sewing materials in one corner.".

"Mother, I don't want this room changed."

"I intend to make new drapes and change it to suit my needs unless you want to use it as an office." She turned, waiting for his response.

He shook his head and backed away.

Mother lowered the fabric. "We'll finish later, Sarie."

Sarie nodded, sent some sort of secret message to Jake's mother, and then slipped out of the room.

Jake stood rooted to the floor. His father had spent his last days here, confined to a bed in a now bare corner. He could feel his father's presence, recall the combination of fear and determination he felt as his father prepared him to take over. The room made him feel trapped. With a muffled sound, he broke free of the spell and headed for the door.

His mother descended from her perch and caught his elbow. "Jake, sit down. I want to talk to you."

He blinked. It sounded like an order. He sat on the nearest leather chair, and his mother sat facing him in the matching chair.

"Son, I've been doing a lot of thinking lately, and I realize we need to make some changes around here."

The ranch was as successful as it had been when his father was alive, and his mother was well cared for. No one had a reason to complain. Nor to want to change things. "Everything is just fine."

"You've tried very hard to take your father's place. But you're not your father."

His gut twisted.

"Nor do any of us want you to be. Seth is dead. You are now owner of this place. Don't you have things you want to do differently?"

Jake hesitated. "I thought of buying a bull from a different breed. Bring in a new blood line."

"Why haven't you?"

His father's orders had kept him from doing so. *If you run the place just like I have, you won't have any problems.* But he didn't say it aloud.

"Jake, I'm as guilty as you are of trying to keep the past alive. Maybe more so." She ducked her head. "I've used you. Created headaches when I didn't have them in order to—" She fluttered her hands. "I'm not even sure why I did it. The headaches were real at first. Sometimes they still are. But they guaranteed I'd get your attention. Then I used them to get my own way." She shuddered. "I can't believe how shallow I was." She sat up straighter. "Hannah made me see how important it is to stand on my own two feet."

Hannah. Her independence had come between them. Now it had spilled over to his mother.

"Jake, I want you to understand that the promises your father exacted from you on his deathbed have been fulfilled. You have taken care of me and your sister better than he could have imagined. You have cared for the ranch as well as he did, if not better. I am hereby releasing you from your promises. I want to be free to move on with my life, and I want you to know you're free to do what you want, both with your life and this ranch." She took his hands. "You need to find someone to share your life with. Go find Hannah. Persuade her you love her and want to *share* your life with her."

"It's not that easy." He bolted from the room and raced for

the barn to saddle his horse and ride from the yard. He bent low over his horse's neck and rode like fury until he reached the top of a distant hill and drew to a stop, staring out at the landscape, though in truth seeing nothing.

His mother had released him from his vow to his father. Said he'd completed it. But was it that easy? He groaned. Hannah was right. He was used to being in control. Could he suddenly let people around him make their own decisions while he stood back? What if they made mistakes? Wouldn't that be his responsibility? What had Hannah said? Just accept people as they are—flaws and all? He did that. Or did he? By wanting to take over their choices, was he saying he didn't accept their way of doing things?

He grunted. Everything he'd done had been to help those he loved. To be the man his father expected him to be. Was he just a shadow of his father? God forbid. "God," he groaned, "what do You expect of me?"

"I have loved thee with an everlasting love: therefore with lovingkindness have I drawn thee."

He let the words of scripture wash over him and through him until he felt cleansed and free. Yes, free. God loved him despite his failures or his successes. With an everlasting love. Could he do any less for his family? For Hannah? How wrong he'd been to try and force her to give up her dreams. She'd never be the sort of woman who contentedly let someone else make all her decisions. He chuckled. He didn't want her to be. He wanted to share his life with a woman who was his equal.

He could not ask her to give up the hotel. In fact—he reined his horse toward home—he'd go to town and give her a hand fixing up the place. If she'd give him a second chance, they'd find a way to work things out so she could keep her hotel.

&

Hannah opened the letter from her grandparents in the post office, read it quickly, and laughed. She'd asked permission to sell the hotel, but they'd written saying they hadn't found what they wanted in California and would come back and take it over themselves. They were arriving tomorrow. She tucked the letter into her pocket and returned to the hotel.

Jake had once offered her a job as companion to his mother. She was prepared to go to the ranch and ask if the offer still stood. But she didn't have time to dwell on the future right now. The hotel demanded her complete and immediate attention.

&

The next day she hurried to the train to meet her grandparents, laughing as her grandfather hugged her right off the ground. Her grandmother kissed her soundly on both cheeks.

"So you've decided you don't want to run a hotel," Grandfather said. "I expect you've found something else you would rather do."

She tucked an arm around each grandparent. "I think so."

Her grandfather squeezed her arm. "I hope he's worthy."

Grandmother and Hannah looked at each other and laughed.

"I want to give him a chance to prove it," Hannah said.

"Do I sense a problem, dear?" Grandmother asked.

"He thinks I'm too independent."

Grandfather snorted. "I guess it's up to you to prove him wrong."

"I hope I can." She hugged them both a little closer. "It's good to have you back."

She let them enter the hotel first and waited for their response to the changes. She'd told them about the fire but wondered if they'd approve of how she'd fixed up the place.

They glanced around. "The rug?" grandmother asked.

"Ruined."

The older woman nodded, went as far as the dining room for a look, and then returned. "It looks fine. We couldn't have done better ourselves."

Hannah gave them one of the bigger rooms upstairs until she could move out of the quarters on the main floor. She left them there to rest.

Partway down the stairs, she saw the door fly open. Jake stood silhouetted in the opening. Her heart finished descending without her then bounced back to her chest to shudder with surprise. She'd been planning to visit him, beg, if necessary, for the offered position. She hadn't expected him to show up in town, brandishing a paintbrush in one hand. Her brain had turned to stone, her tongue refused to work. Finally one thought surfaced. "What do you want?"

He waved the paintbrush. "I'll help you fix the hotel."

She took the rest of the steps. She couldn't stop staring at him. "It's all done." She waved her hand to indicate the surroundings.

His eager expression flattened, and he dropped his hand to his side. "Oh." He seemed to consider the facts. "Guess I'm too late."

"It's done," she repeated, unable to think what it meant that he'd come, offering to help.

"Well then. That's good. And the business is doing well?"

"Yes." She remembered she wanted to ask him about the position. "Jake, remember you asked me to be your mother's companion. Is the offer still open?"

"Huh? Oh. No. She doesn't need a companion."

"I see." She held her breath against the disappointment

ripping through her chest.

"Hannah, I've changed my mind about a lot of things." He stepped aside as one of the guests came through the door. "Can we go someplace and talk?"

She hesitated. Could she stand any more announcements from him? And yet she followed him outside, allowing him to take her hand. He paused, glanced up and down the street, and then led her north to the church.

"We can talk privately here," he said.

They sat together on a pew. *Lord,* she prayed, *give me strength to accept this.*

He took her hand and turned to look into her face.

She kept her emotions buried. She would not reveal her pain, her weakness.

He studied her intensely. "Hannah, I've changed."

She nodded, though she had no idea what he meant.

"You were right," he continued. "I felt I was responsible for everyone. I couldn't let go for fear something would go wrong and I'd be to blame. You see, my father made me promise on his deathbed that I would take care of everything and do just as he would."

Again she nodded, still no closer to understanding.

"I realize I have fulfilled my vow to my father. I expect it will take a little practice to actually live what I decided, but from now on, I'm determined to let people make their own choices." He played with the collar of her dress. "If you want to run a hotel, that's up to you. I just want what's best for you." He sought her gaze, his eyes filled with longing and uncertainty. "I accept you, Hannah. Just as you are."

At her surprised blink, he hurried on, as if he felt he had to explain his whole plan, and she let him. She had to know exactly what he had in mind before she spoke.

"I don't want to run your life. I want to share it. You see, it was your independence that attracted me from the first. It challenged my idea that I had to be in control. You taught me how to let go of my overwhelming sense of responsibility. If you'll have me, we'll find a way to work things out so you can continue to run your hotel. I'll even help you."

Her whole being wanted to explode with joy. "I've let the hotel go."

"Go? Where?"

She giggled. "Nowhere, silly. I've turned the ownership back to my grandparents. They take over tomorrow."

His expression fell. "You're going back East?"

She smiled at his disappointment. "I had hoped I could still be your mother's companion, but you say the position is closed."

He chuckled. "Seems like you taught her the benefits of independence."

"That leaves me without a position." She lowered her head so he wouldn't see the longing, the hope, or the beginning of joy in her eyes.

He lifted her chin and waited until she met his look.

When she saw the way he studied her, his eyes dark with love and promise, tears stung the backs of her eyes.

"Hannah Williams, I love you. Do you care for me just a little? Do you think you could learn to love me?"

She whooped. "Jake Sperling, I love you so much now I can hardly think." She threw her arms around his neck and raised her face for a kiss.

epilogue

Hannah adjusted her veil. It shimmered exactly as she had once dreamed it would.

"You're almost as beautiful as your grandmother was the day I married her," Grandfather said as he waited to escort her down the aisle.

She had decided to stay at the hotel until the wedding to help her grandparents get settled back in. Even though Hannah missed Jake when he had to be away, she appreciated the time spent with her grandparents. Their love for each other and support for her meant a lot. She kissed her grandfather's cheek. "I wish Mother would have come, but I'm awfully glad you and Grandmother are here."

Audrey peeked around the corner, giving them a commentary. "Mother and your grandmother have been seated." She turned to her sons. "You two are next. Now remember what I said. No running. No yelling. Walk quietly up to Uncle Jake and stand at his side."

"Yes, Momma," Luke said and took Sammy's hand.

Hannah kissed them both on their cheeks before they headed down the aisle. They made it halfway before they broke into a run.

Jake caught them as they reached the front and steadied them into position, their freshly scrubbed faces looking cherubic against the backdrop of a lovely floral arrangement.

Audrey went next, her pale pink dress swishing around her

ankles as she walked. She took her place at the front and turned to wait for Hannah.

"It's our turn, little girl," Grandfather said.

She nodded and took her grandfather's arm. Even though she was glad her grandfather was there, she couldn't help but wish for a moment that it was her father escorting her down the aisle to her future.

She'd told Jake how she'd come to realize that it was acceptance she longed for more than independence. She'd confessed she'd sold her prized possession, her father's pocket watch. Jake had surprised her by presenting it as a wedding present. He had bought it back for her. Oh, how she loved this man.

She met Jake's eyes and forgot everything else as Grandfather escorted her to his side.

Pastor Rawson smiled at them and began the service by reading scriptures reminding them that marriage was a holy institution. "What therefore God hath joined together, let not man put asunder." He then began the vows. "Do you, Jake, take this woman—"

Jake squeezed Hannah's hand, silently assuring her of his intention to honor the till-death-do-us-part words.

Suddenly the vase of flowers at Pastor Rawson's side crashed to the floor, soaking the poor man.

A few splashes hit Hannah in the face, and she wiped them off.

Luke shoved Sammy to the floor. "It's your fault. You pushed me."

Sammy came up sputtering and flailing his arms. "Did not."

"Boys," Audrey warned.

Harvey, Jake's best man, grabbed for Luke, but the boy

skidded out of reach and raced down the aisle, Sammy hot on his heels.

"They're your boys," Audrey muttered to Harvey. "You go get them."

Hannah giggled. She glanced over her shoulder and saw Jake's mother press the back of her wrist to her forehead.

Mrs. Sperling caught her watching and looked embarrassed before she sat up straight and ignored the screaming pair of boys.

Hannah glanced at her grandparents, who smiled widely and likewise ignored the commotion.

Jake drew her closer and leaned over to speak so the pastor could hear, "Let's get this done before they bring the place down around our ears."

Amid the sound of two rambunctious little boys, the embarrassment of a set of parents, and the obvious glee of her grandparents, Hannah and Jake promised to love and honor each other always.

A Letter To Our Readers

Dear Reader:

In order that we might better contribute to your reading enjoyment, we would appreciate your taking a few minutes to respond to the following questions. We welcome your comments and read each form and letter we receive. When completed, please return to the following:

Fiction Editor
Heartsong Presents
PO Box 719
Uhrichsville, Ohio 44683

1. Did you enjoy reading *The Dreams of Hannah Williams* by Linda Ford?
   ❑ Very much! I would like to see more books by this author!
   ❑ Moderately. I would have enjoyed it more if

   _____

   _____

   _____

2. Are you a member of **Heartsong Presents**? ❑ Yes ❑ No
   If no, where did you purchase this book? _____

   _____

3. How would you rate, on a scale from 1 (poor) to 5 (superior), the cover design? _____

4. On a scale from 1 (poor) to 10 (superior), please rate the following elements.

   _____ Heroine   _____ Plot
   _____ Hero   _____ Inspirational theme
   _____ Setting   _____ Secondary characters

5. These characters were special because? _____

_____

_____

6. How has this book inspired your life? _____

_____

_____

7. What settings would you like to see covered in future
   Heartsong Presents books? _____

_____

_____

8. What are some inspirational themes you would like to see
   treated in future books? _____

_____

_____

9. Would you be interested in reading other **Heartsong
   Presents** titles? ❏ Yes ❏ No

10. Please check your age range:
     ❏ Under 18   ❏ 18-24
     ❏ 25-34   ❏ 35-45
     ❏ 46-55   ❏ Over 55

Name _____

Occupation _____

Address _____

City, State, Zip_____

KENTUCKY *Brides*

3 stories in 1

Three Kentucky women find that life isn't anything like they expected. Stories are by authors Lauralee Bliss, Irene B. Brand, and Yvonne Lehman.

Historical, paperback, 352 pages, 5³/₁₆" x 8"

Heart♥ng

Any 12
Heartsong
Presents titles
for only
$27.00*

HISTORICAL ROMANCE IS CHEAPER BY THE DOZEN!

Buy any assortment of twelve *Heartsong Presents* titles and save 25% off of the already discounted price of $2.97 each!

*plus $3.00 shipping and handling per order and sales tax where applicable.
If outside the U.S. please call
740-922-7280 for shipping charges.

HEARTSONG PRESENTS TITLES AVAILABLE NOW:

(If ordering from this page, please remember to include it with the order form.)

Presents

103
69
63

♡

HEARTSONG
PRESENTS

If you love Christian romance…

$10.⁹⁹

You'll love Heartsong Presents' inspiring and faith-filled romances by today's very best Christian authors. . .Wanda E. Brunstetter, Mary Connealy, Susan Page Davis, Cathy Marie Hake, and Joyce Livingston, to mention a few!

When you join Heartsong Presents, you'll enjoy four brand-new, mass market, 176-page books—two contemporary and two historical—that will build you up in your faith when you discover God's role in every relationship you read about!

Imagine. . .four new romances every four weeks—with men and women like you who long to meet the one God has chosen as the love of their lives…all for the low price of $10.99 postpaid.

Mass Market 176 Pages

To join, simply visit www.heartsong presents.com or complete the coupon below and mail it to the address provided.

✂ -

YES! Sign me up for Heart♥ng!

NEW MEMBERSHIPS WILL BE SHIPPED IMMEDIATELY!
Send no money now. We'll bill you only $10.99 postpaid with your first shipment of four books. Or for faster action, call 1-740-922-7280.

NAME _____

ADDRESS_____

CITY_____ STATE _____ ZIP _____

MAIL TO: HEARTSONG PRESENTS, P.O. Box 721, Uhrichsville, Ohio 44683
or sign up at **WWW.HEARTSONGPRESENTS.COM**